Iron Eyes Makes War

The infamous bounty hunter, Iron Eyes, is forced to chase the wanted outlaw Joe Brewster down into an arid desert even though he has been badly wounded in a showdown with Brewster's brothers.

Losing his pony, Iron Eyes is forced to follow on foot. To his surprise, he discovers an oasis in a valley. Iron Eyes trails the outlaw into the valley and soon finds that a few families are living there under threat of death by Don Miguel Sanchez and his army of vaqueros.

Will Iron Eyes leave or fight until the bloody showdown?

Iron Eyes Makes War

RORY BLACK

A Black Horse Western

ROBERT HALE · LONDON

ISBN 978-0-7090-8810-3

Robert Hale Limited
Clerkenwell House
Clerkenwell Green
London EC1R 0HT

www.halebooks.com

Typeset by
Derek Doyle & Associates, Shaw Heath
Printed and bound in Great Britain by
CPI Antony Rowe, Chippenham and Eastbourne

*Dedicated with love to Alexia Rose,
my first grandchild.*

PROLOGUE

The three ruthless outlaws had stayed outside the boundaries of San Remas for more than two hours since arriving in Johnson County. Each of the Brewster brothers had remained silent for most of the time they had rested their mounts upon the wooded hillside above the small prosperous town. Their high vantage point gave them uninterrupted views across most of the wide landscape set below them. They could see the cattle out on the lush, fertile range to the east of the town and the trail which led through Deadman's Gulch towards the distant border with Mexico. The sun was now setting and the brothers began to ready themselves.

Each of them threw his saddle on to the back of his well watered mount, then secured the cinch straps. The eyes of the younger brothers Clem and Joe were never far from their older, more seasoned sibling. Frank Brewster stepped into his stirrup, hauled himself atop his horse and glanced at his small but loyal gang. He swung his grey round and faced his brothers. He watched as they mounted and gathered up their reins.

'Remember, boys,' he began, 'Me and Clem go into the bank and Joe clears the street.'

Clem cleared his throat. 'What if we gets split up, Frank?'

Frank lowered his head and looked at his saddle horn. 'If'n we do get separated we all meet up in Rio Valdo at the Longhorn. We has us a good time and then we head south down into Mexico. You can buy a whole lot more down there with silver dollars or greenbacks.'

The younger brothers smiled. His words had given them confidence and it showed. They waited for Frank to spur his mount into a trot, then followed him out of the brush and down the steep hillside towards the unsuspecting town. The Brewsters were new to bank robberies, yet they had taken to it well. This would be only the fifth time they had attempted to separate a bank from its money but the project held no fear for any of them. The previous four bank robberies had gone well, without any mistakes, but it had earned each of them a price on his head. A price which had caught the attention of many bounty hunters, including the most deadly hunter of men in the West. Although the Brewsters did not know it, Iron Eyes was already on their trail.

The riders rode into the town with casual ease. They remained a few yards apart as they proceeded along the narrow main street towards the red-brick structure set midway along the 200-yard stretch. The word 'bank' lured them like moths to a flame.

There was barely an hour's daylight left. More than enough for the outlaws to do their worst. Twenty or so mounts were tied up along the street. Frank looked to Joe and nodded. Joe knew what that signal meant. He never entered the banks. His was a more specialized job. A more dangerous job. Probably far more dangerous than robbing the bank with cocked guns in hands. He had to remain mounted and clear the streets. He would wait for his two partners in crime to enter the bank, then ensure that all the townspeople's horses were run off. He also had to fire his guns up and down the street when his brothers came out of the bank, to ensure that they could make a clean escape from the town.

The horsemen drew rein directly opposite the bank, beneath the canopy of a proud tree. Clem dismounted first and firmly knotted his reins around a hitching pole. He loosened his bandanna so that he could easily raise it to cover the lower part of his face. Frank Brewster glanced up and down the street. It was far busier than he had expected. Men, women and children were going about their late afternoon rituals but these meant nothing to the hardened outlaw. He dropped from his saddle, tied his reins and then turned to face the bank.

'C'mon, Clem,' Frank drawled. 'Let's get this done.'

Both men pulled their empty saddle-bags from behind their saddle cantles. They walked with cold purpose towards the red-brick building as their brother rode back down the street to cut the reins of every horse within view.

It took less than ten minutes to achieve their goal after Joe had started to fire his guns and clear the streets of anyone who might prove problematic.

Frank and Clem came rushing from the bank with their heavily laden bags over their shoulders. Frank drew one of his guns and added to the confusion by shooting blindly at store fronts. Without a second thought he aimed and fired at a woman and child. Both fell limply on the boardwalk.

Clem pulled both his own and his brother's reins free from the hitching pole as Frank fired the last of his bullets into the glass pane of the bank's door. With the stench of gunsmoke hanging in the air the outlaws continued to empty their guns at anyone on the street. They did not care who or what they killed in order to escape with their loot.

The sound of glass shattering and people screaming resounded as all three horsemen spurred and thundered out of the town. A town that was red with the blood of innocents.

Dust rose into the darkening sky as another rider reached the top of the hillside where the three brothers had waited for so long. Iron Eyes stopped his pony and looked down at the scene far below him.

He could just make out the fleeing trio of riders, who were galloping south. The bounty hunter steadied his mount and listened to the pitiful wailing far below him within the streets of San Remas.

Iron Eyes spurred and aimed the pony at the town. He would soon discover for himself what new atrocities the ruthless men he hunted had just perpetrated.

ONE

Rio Valdo was a sleepy town balanced on the very edge of humanity. It had once been part of pre-revolution Mexico but over the ensuing generations had somehow found itself on the other side of the unmarked border. Now claimed to be part of the Lone Star State it even had a sheriff who wore a Stetson. Yet the majority of those who lived in or around the remote settlement still favoured sombreros. A few Texan rituals had taken root but the overall flavour of Rio Valdo remained Latin in origin. As the sun dipped beyond the distant mountains a red glow erupted across the cloudless heavens.

It was as though the very sky was on fire. It should have been regarded as an omen. An omen of impending bloodshed.

For with the dying embers of the fiery sunset on his back the lone rider drew closer to the town to which he had tracked his prey. As the spectral horseman reached the first of the settlements buildings he could see the eyes of those who feared him. They were many.

There was no mistaking the man atop the dishevelled Indian pony who steered his mount towards the mixture of whitewashed adobes and more recently constructed red-brick buildings. His was a description which nobody ever forgot. Some thought that the stories of the bounty hunter were exaggerations. Those who had set eyes upon him knew that they were in fact the truth. If pain had a face it was his. A lifetime of hunting creatures of all kinds had left their scars upon not only his body but his face as well. Every battle he had fought was carved into the twisted flesh of his face. The residents of the remote town fled as he rode into the outskirts of Rio Valdo. The deeply religious and superstitious had set eyes upon death in human form. If there had been a church it would have been filled to overflowing with the terrified.

Yet Iron Eyes knew what he was. He was simply a hunter.

He was considered by the Apaches to be a ghost. A man who could never be killed because he no longer lived. The majority of white men whom he had encountered thought he had to be an Indian. Their logic was that only an Indian could track his prey so ruthlessly. Only an Indian would take so much pleasure in capturing and killing those with bounty on their heads. Another reason that white folks considered him not to be one of them was his mane of long black hair, which had never come close to a barber's scissors. His scarred face had never required shaving in all his long days.

Iron Eyes knew only one thing for certain. He was unwelcome wherever he went. He was hated and feared with equal venom by nearly everyone. But most of those who feared him were wanted, dead or alive.

They had the greatest reason to be afraid. For once he had your wanted poster in his deep trail-coat pockets, he would never quit his hunt until you were dead and he had claimed the bounty.

Even though Iron Eyes had never been to Rio Valdo before, his name was being spoken by all those who saw his brutalized features as he spurred his pony deep into the town. One voice became a hundred. They were all chanting the unholy name of Iron Eyes. The crimson rays of the setting sun reflected off the windows of the buildings as he approached. It made the bounty hunter look as though he were the Devil himself, set amid mythical flames.

Women hauled their young off the streets. Grown men felt their hearts quicken as the emaciated horseman studied them all with interest. For Iron Eyes had the scent of his prey in his flared nostrils. He was on the look-out for three wanted outlaws who were worth more than $5,000. Men in sombreros on the boardwalks crossed themselves in silent gratitude to their Maker as he passed them.

Halfway along the crooked main street Iron Eyes drew rein.

His head moved as his eyes darted around the quiet town at those who fearfully watched him from the blackest of shadows. He then looked up at the newly painted façade atop the porch overhang directly before him. The dying sun danced across its still fresh paintwork.

It had only one word upon it.

'Sheriff!' Iron Eyes read aloud.

He saw a lamp being lit inside the office through its solitary window. He nodded to himself, threw his long right leg over the neck of his tired pony and slid to the ground. He led the animal to the full trough outside the office and tied his reins firmly to a wooden upright. The pony began to drink. It was the first time it had tasted water in nearly twenty miles of hard riding.

Iron Eyes stepped up on to the boardwalk and turned to face the street. Lights were being lit all along the main thoroughfare as cantinas, cafés and saloons acknowledged the coming of yet another night. His thin left hand slid down into a pocket of his battered and torn jacket and retrieved a slim cigar. He placed it between his teeth.

Then behind him he heard the sound of a match being ignited by a thumbnail.

The tall bounty hunter turned quickly and stared into the darkness at the seated figure. The flame lit up the face of the man, who appeared to be at least

15

sixty with a proud, grey, handlebar moustache. It was the first face he had encountered in Rio Valdo which showed no fear.

'Light?' the man asked.

Iron Eyes did not reply. He walked the two steps to the man and leaned over. He sucked in the flame and then allowed the smoke to dwell for a while in his lungs.

'Much obliged.' Iron Eyes said as he straightened up.

The man produced a corncob pipe and gripped its stem between what was left of his teeth. He touched the flame to the bowl and then tossed the match away.

'You Iron Eyes?' the old man asked through a cloud of smoke.

The bounty hunter narrowed his eyes and then leaned against the red-brick wall. He continued to watch the man, who puffed on the aromatic pipe.

'You're mighty smart for an old-timer.'

'Not really,' the man disagreed. 'I heard about you a whole heap of times from folks on both sides of the law. Never thought them stories about you could be true but, setting eyes on you as close as this, I reckon they are.'

Iron Eyes inhaled the smoked of his cigar deeply. 'I figure that I must kinda stand out from the average varmint.'

'Yep!' the man agreed. 'Never thought anyone could be as ugly as them tales said you was. Damned

16

if'n you ain't even uglier.'

Iron Eyes nodded.

'Ya ain't afraid of me then?'

The man laughed. 'Nope.'

'How come?'

'I'm the sheriff!' the man pulled his coat apart to reveal the tin star pinned to his vest. 'You ain't gonna get ornery with the law. I'm the critter who has to dish out the reward money when you bring in your kill. Right?'

'Ya damn smart,' Iron Eyes looked at the door. 'Who ya got in there, Sheriff? I seen the lamp light up as I hauled rein.'

'Just my deputy.'

'Is he any good?'

'Makes the worst coffee this side of the Rio Grande but he keeps the office clean,' The man grinned.

Iron Eyes tilted his head and blew a line of smoke at the ground. 'Ya know my handle, what's your name?'

'Drew Colby.'

The tall man walked to the very edge of the boardwalk. He rested a shoulder on the nearest upright and stared through the cigar smoke out at the street and the people who were keeping well clear of him.

'Ya had three riders come into town in the last day or so, Sheriff Colby?'

'Yep!' The man eased himself up from the

hardback chair and moved to the side of the figure who was at least a foot taller than he was. He looked up at the features which grew even more horrific as the very last of the sun's crimson rays shed an ominous gleam directly into the scarred face. 'They wanted dead or alive?'

'Yep.'

'I figured as much.' Sheriff Drew Colby nodded. 'You don't chase outlaws who ain't, I hear.'

'Ya hear right. I don't cotton to prisoners.'

Colby laughed. He had never met anyone as blunt about his work as the bounty hunter obviously was.

'Reckon there ain't no point in me trying to tell you not to go shooting them Navy Colts in town, is there?' The lawman sighed as he tapped his pipe against the upright.

'Not hardly.' Iron Eyes rubbed his neck and shook his long limp hair like a hound dog trying to shake rain from its back. 'I don't see their horses anywhere along the street.'

The sheriff pointed to the far end of town. A lantern was just being lit outside the livery stable.

'They rode to the livery when they arrived. Their horses must still be up there.'

'Where'd they go?' Iron Eyes asked.

Again Colby pointed. This time to the nearest of the saloons.

'The Longhorn saloon. I seen them head in there about two or three hours back, Iron Eyes. I ain't seen them come out.'

'Got girls in there?'

'Yep.' Colby smiled. 'Pretty Mexican girls. The kind that makes a man wish he was twenty years younger.'

The statement meant nothing to the tall bounty hunter. He just nodded and stared at the building as though memorizing its every plank of wood. Iron Eyes sucked the last of the smoke from his cigar, then tossed the last half-inch away. He pulled the crumpled posters from his pocket and handed them to the lawman.

'This'll tell you all about the critters I'm gunnin' for.'

Sheriff Colby turned and walked to the office door. He opened it and moved to the lamp on his desk. He did not see the shocked expression etched on the face of his young deputy as Iron Eyes followed the lawman into the light. Colby tilted the Wanted posters until the amber lamplight was upon them. He read and then looked at the tall man beside him. The bounty hunter was like a carved wooden statue. There was hardly any expression on the twisted face. Only the eyes moved as they surveyed everything, looking for potential danger.

'The Brewster brothers?' Colby questioned. 'Is that who them critters were?'

Iron Eyes nodded. 'Clem, Frank and Joe.'

'They held up a few banks up north, huh?' Colby commented. 'Is that why you're after them?'

'They killed a few folks over in San Remas as well,' Iron Eyes added. 'I don't cotton to grown men who kill females for the fun of it.'

'What kinda females we talking about?'

'It don't matter none.' Iron Eyes pulled the guns which he had tucked into his pants belt and checked them. Only when satisfied that they were fully loaded did he return them to his belt.

'It's bin a while since I seen me a pair of Navy Colts, boy.' the sheriff said. 'Most men use .45s. How come you use .36s?'

'They're light.' Iron Eyes was about to turn away when he caught sight of the dumbfounded deputy's reflection in the window. He glanced at the youth who could not have been more than sixteen. 'I ain't seen a deputy look so young before, Sheriff.'

'Ain't many grown men want the job.' Colby shrugged.

Iron Eyes looked hard at the deputy. 'What they call ya?'

'Johnny Ryker,' the deputy gulped and stammered.

'Always watch your back, Johnny Ryker,' Iron Eyes advised. 'Most people get killed by cowards. Cowards like to shoot folks in the back. Remember that and you might get as old as the sheriff.'

The youth nodded. 'Yes, sir.'

Colby pointed at the guns whose grips were pointing out from the tall man's slim waist.

'By all the stories I've heard about you, boy, I'd

have thought you'd have the fanciest shooting rig going. How come you ain't got a gunbelt and holsters?'

'Ain't never needed them.' Iron Eyes walked back out into the darkness. His eyes screwed up as he focused across the street on to the saloon again.

Sheriff Colby leaned on the office door with his deputy staring over his shoulder.

'Reckon it's time, huh?'

'Yep. It's time.' Iron Eyes stepped down on to the sand and started to walk directly towards the smell of stale sawdust and the sound of a tinny piano.

The Longhorn was busy, as always. Those who had witnessed the arrival of the infamous bounty hunter had not ventured into the saloon to inform those inside. They had done what all sane men and women would do when seeing Iron Eyes and headed back to their homes.

Iron Eyes studied the two-storey building as he approached. It had a veranda with a low rail which stretched the entire length of its front. Four windows faced the main street. Only three of them had lights flickering behind their lace drapes. Two larger windows were set to either side of the saloon's swing doors. Their panes were covered in painted images to prevent the innocent from seeing within.

The experienced hunter of men looked back at the windows above the veranda. He knew what was probably happening up in those rooms. And he also knew that the Brewster brothers were probably occupying them with a little female company. They would be celebrating their latest triumph.

Since he had set out after the outlaws he had never been this close to them before. He had never been close enough to their hoof dust for them even to imagine that they were being trailed by the most lethal bounty hunter in the West.

He stepped up on to the boardwalk, paused and then looked over the swing doors into the smoke-filled interior. His bullet-coloured eyes narrowed. A dozen or more tables were crowded with men playing cards. Scores of other men were resting against the long bar counter as if afraid to venture too far away from the bartenders. A pair of bar girls in skimpy dresses moved around between the saloon's patrons trying to find their next paying customers.

Iron Eyes rested a bony hand on top of the swing doors. He continued to stare into the room like an eagle trying to locate his chosen prey. Close to the saloon's back wall he noticed a staircase which led up to a landing. It looked as though there were more rooms towards the rear of the building. A door up on the landing opened and a drunken man staggered out with a rather rotund female. Most of her face-paint was now covering the man's face as they both navigated their way down the stairs back to the heart of the drinking-hole.

That was where the outlaws were, Iron Eyes

silently told himself. The three Brewster's were otherwise occupied. A cruel smile crossed his mangled features. That would make killing them easier.

He nodded to himself and put another cigar between his teeth before pushing the door inwards. He had barely taken two strides across the sawdust when he noticed that the piano player had ceased pounding the ivories. Every eye was upon him as he strode toward the bar.

Men of all shapes and sizes watched the strange, unholy-looking figure as he walked to the tune of his spurs. Each of the onlookers was silent.

Iron Eyes noticed how men parted and allowed him to reach the bar. He placed a boot on the brass rail, then looked to both sides. Men backed away without even realizing that they had done so. Even the bar girls did not approach. For what seemed an eternity Iron Eyes waited. At last one of the bartenders summoned the courage to move to him.

'How can I help you, stranger?'

'Whiskey,' Iron Eyes said. 'An unopened bottle with a label on it.'

As the bartender went to get a bottle Iron Eyes pulled a match from his pocket and struck it across one of his gun grips. He cupped its flame and sucked in the smoke before dropping the match into a spittoon.

The entire saloon was hushed in silence.

When the bottle and thimble-glass were placed

before the bounty hunter Iron Eyes placed a silver coin upon the bar top, then pulled the cork. He lifted the bottle and drank from its neck. He took three long swallows, then he pushed the cork back and slid the bottle into one of his deep pockets.

'I'm looking for the Brewsters,' Iron Eyes exclaimed.

Without even realizing it, one of the bartenders looked up to the landing. The gaunt figure nodded at the man as though he had actually told him the answer to his question. He then began the long walk around the bar counter towards the staircase.

With one fluid action, Iron Eyes pulled one of his deadly guns and cocked its hammer. He slowly ascended the stairs towards the landing like a panther closing in on its prey.

Only his spurs made any sound.

Every single person in the saloon watched. Most had open mouths. All knew that at any moment they would hear the noise of lethal lead come from above them. They all realized it would be far safer to leave the saloon, yet none of them could tear themselves away from knowing who would be victorious in the forthcoming gunfight.

Iron Eyes reached the landing. He turned. His eyes darted across the open space to the four doors. Each had a number painted upon its wooden surface.

The sound of boisterous exercise was coming from two of the rooms, whilst the others were silent.

The bounty hunter walked to the line of doors. They were roughly ten feet apart. With the gun pointing from his hip, Iron Eyes leaned close to the first door and strained to hear.

There was no noise. His mind raced as he tried to recall which of the windows he had observed from the street had not had a light behind its drape. He remembered, and moved to the next door. He stared at the number 'two'. This time he did not have to strain to hear. The sound of bed springs and grunting made it obvious that at least one of the outlaws was inside.

He glanced at the remaining two doors.

When the shooting started, he knew that the other brothers would soon come out with guns blazing.

Iron Eyes inhaled, drew the other gun and cocked its hammer to match the one already primed. He sucked in smoke and then raised his bony left leg.

The sound of the door being kicked off its hinges echoed around the Longhorn. Iron Eyes took only half a step forward and saw the head of the eldest Brewster rise from the thick quilted bedcovers. The face stared at him as the female began to scream. She was obviously not quite as drunk as Frank Brewster. She could see who had just destroyed the door.

'Brewster?' the bounty hunter drawled through cigar smoke.

The outlaw desperately clambered across the hysterical female and the bed towards the holstered gun in the fancy shooting rig on a worm-eaten stool.

Like a cat playing with a mouse, Iron Eyes waited the fraction of a second it took for Frank Brewster to pull the Remington free of its holster before he squeezed his own triggers.

A deafening *rat-a-tat* filled the upper floor of the Longhorn. Both of Iron Eye's bullets hit the outlaw in the neck. Blood splattered over the bed and the female before Frank Brewster slid to the floor taking the sheets with him. The bar girl was naked and covered in blood. Upon seeing what covered her pale flesh she fainted.

Iron Eyes heard both of the doors to the other rooms opening. He swung around and saw the first man with his guns in his hands. Iron Eyes instantly recognized the face as matching the picture on the Wanted poster. This was Clem Brewster, his memory told him. The outlaw fired his weaponry. Two bullets hit the doorframe. A million splinters showered over Iron Eyes, filling his eyes with hot, burning debris. He staggered as the noise of two more screaming women filled the upper storey of the Longhorn.

Instinctively Iron Eyes returned fire. He watched through half-closed eyes as the youngest of the outlaws flew backwards and landed at the feet of his stunned brother.

Joe Brewster ducked into the room as Iron Eyes

fired again.

Iron Eyes spat the cigar from his mouth and pushed one of his guns into his belt. He cocked the hammer of his .36 with one hand as his other frantically tried to rid his eyes of the agonizing splinters which were burning into them.

He was panting as he managed to rid his eyes of most of the splinters. He dropped low and looked back along the landing. Steam rose from the two bullet holes in the half-naked body but there was no sign of the last of the outlaws.

'I'm gonna kill you, Joe!' Iron Eyes yelled. There was no reply from behind the furthermost door.

Then he heard the sound of breaking glass coming from the room. Iron Eyes drew back to his full height and ran to the closed door. He kicked it open. He squinted into the lamplit room and saw that the drapes were floating in the evening breeze. A terrified female knelt behind the bed, sobbing. Behind her he could see the broken window.

Iron Eyes raced across the room, leapt over the bed and landed next to the naked women. He poked his gun out of the window and then his head. He just had time to see the outlaw drop from the balcony to the street below.

'Damn it all!' Iron Eyes growled. 'Some critters just don't know when to quit living.'

Iron Eyes scrambled out of the window in fevered pursuit of his prey. He ran across the balcony just in time to see the half-naked outlaw pause at the corner of a building with the word 'Bank' emblazoned upon its façade.

Iron Eyes saw the gunsmoke and then felt the bullet hit him in the left trail-coat pocket. The sound of the whiskey bottle shattering filled his ears, and the liquor soaked through the coarse fabric. He raised a gun but saw the outlaw disappear beneath the overhangs.

'Git back here, ya yella dog!'

Iron Eyes lifted a long leg over the railings and jumped from the balcony. He hit the ground hard as two more bullets cut through the darkness and passed within inches of him.

Joe Brewster was headed for the livery, the bounty hunter told himself. He had only just begun to make chase when he was knocked off his feet by what felt like a mule kick. He had been hit. The bullet had caught him in the ribs.

Iron Eyes lay on his back beneath a street lantern. Then heard a sound he recognized.

The sound of a horse thundering away.

He rolled on to his knees and watched his blood dripping into the sand as a shadow traced across him.

'Need a hand, Iron Eyes?'

The wounded bounty hunter glanced through his long limp hair up at the sheriff.

'Yep,' Iron Eyes muttered.

TWO

Pungent whiskey fumes hung around Iron Eyes from the broken bottle in his deep trail-coat pocket. Although powerful it masked the other aroma which the bounty hunter wore like a badge of his profession. The smell of death. Iron Eyes had refused to submit to the pain which racked his emaciated body as he staggered towards the livery stable building that stood at the very end of the main street. The wily sheriff kept pace with the bounty hunter and chewed on his pipe stem silently. He was amazed that the younger man was even conscious, let alone capable of walking.

When they reached the stables bathed in the illumination of two street lanterns, Iron Eyes stopped and stared at the ground just outside the wide-open doors of the livery.

'What you seen?' Colby enquired with a slight tilt of his head.

29

'Tracks,' Iron Eyes retorted. 'What the hell else would I see, Sheriff?'

Colby shrugged and poked both hands in his coat pockets. He shivered against the night air and looked back down the street towards the Longhorn.

'You kill the other two?'

'Yep.' Iron Eyes knelt and ran a bony hand over the churned-up ground. 'Killed 'em dead.'

Sheriff Colby shook his shoulders as though trying to fend off the night chill. He could not understand how the frail-looking Iron Eyes appeared not to have noticed the change in temperature since sundown.

'What you looking there for anyways, boy?' the lawman asked. 'I bet a dozen or more wagons and horses bin across that piece of dirt today. You ain't gonna find nothing.'

Iron Eyes glanced up at the whiskered man. 'I've bin hunting all my life, old-timer. I can see things here that most folks would never notice.'

Sheriff Colby watched his companion return to his full height. 'Yeah? What can you see in that chunk of dirt?'

Iron Eyes raised a scarred eyebrow. 'I can see that Joe Brewster took both the saddle-bags out of there on the neck of his horse when he lit out..'

Colby edged closer to the wounded man. 'What saddle-bags?'

'The ones filled with money, Sheriff.' Iron Eyes turned and walked into the dark interior of the building. Only the glowing embers of the blacksmith's forge lit up the vast wooden structure. The eyes of a score of horses gleamed from the shadows of their stalls cast by the forge's eerie red light.

The lawman trailed Iron Eyes into the livery. 'What money we talking about, boy?'

Iron Eyes looked at the sheriff. 'The money they stole from the bank up at San Remas.'

Colby scratched his neck. 'If that's right, they must have left the bags in here whilst they went down to the saloon.'

Iron Eyes nodded slowly. 'Yep. They sure must have.'

'You telling me that them outlaws left their saddle-bags – saddle-bags filled with loot, in this old barn?' The sheriff looked confused. 'I mean, they could have bin stolen by anyone who cottoned to them.'

'Yep.' Slowly Iron Eyes strolled towards the warm forge, put a cigar between his teeth and leaned over. The coals were still mighty hot. He sucked in the smoke and then turned to face the sheriff. Pain was carved into his twisted features.

'That's dumb,' Colby added.

'Didn't say the Brewsters were smart.' The bounty hunter exhaled a long line of smoke through his teeth. 'I just said they was outlaws.'

Colby walked towards the tall figure. He could see the blood on the trail-coat. The closer he got

31

the more blood he could see upon the bounty hunter's sodden shirt and pants leg.

'You need tending, Iron Eyes. You ain't just bleeding, you're pumping, boy.'

Iron Eyes sucked hard on the cigar, as though the smoke might stop the pain. 'Ya could be right. I figure two of my ribs are busted.'

The sheriff lifted the side of the long, stained coat away from the brutal injury and stared at it hard and long. 'Only two ribs?'

'Maybe three.' Iron Eyes smiled defiantly. 'I've had me a lot of ribs shot up over the years. Hard to be exact.'

Colby swallowed hard. His eyes focused on the bones protruding from the thin man's side amid the blood. His eyes went up to the scarred face.

'That's gotta hurt something awful.'

Iron Eyes nodded. 'Yep.'

Sheriff Colby pulled at the sleeve of the tall man. 'C'mon. I'll take you to Doc Harper. He'll fix you up. Reckon given a few days' rest you'll can be back on the trail of that Brewster varmint again.'

Iron Eyes started back for the tall doors. 'I'll be on his trail before midnight.'

Colby was about to disagree when he saw the determined expression on the face of the bounty hunter as the moonlight hit it. There was something in that twisted face that told him that Iron Eyes meant every word.

*

Dust blew continuously across the rolling landscape all around him; there seemed to be nothing to fill the rider's lungs except dry choking air. The Indian pony was labouring beneath its master as the rider's sharp spurs drove into its flesh for the umpteenth time. Attempting to outrun the vicious blood-covered spurs the pony raced down through a small wood back into the blazing sun and the arid terrain which seemed to roll on to the almost featureless distant horizon.

The rider's vicious wound had been sewn up and his narrow body wrapped like an ancient Egyptian mummy but the pain remained constant. Like his pony he was trying vainly to outrun his own agony. Racing along a dry arroya Iron Eyes dragged on his reins and brought the exhausted animal to an abrupt halt.

The pony was about to fall when the bounty hunter leapt from his saddle, knelt and stared at the hard, unforgiving ground. Even his seasoned hunting prowess had been tested for the previous ten miles. He ran the palm of a hand across the surface of the ground and then sighed heavily. If there were tracks, he could not see them any longer.

They had been blown away, like everything else in this brutal arid place.

Iron Eyes stood upright, wrapped the long ends of the reins around his left hand and started to walk. With every step of his long thin legs the man with the matted mane of black hair kept looking all around him for any hint of his prey. But there was none.

Joe Brewster seemed to have vanished into thin air.

The bounty hunter knew that it was impossible for anyone to escape him. Nobody had ever managed that feat. He had always been able to track down the outlaws and gain the bounty money on their heads.

His bullet-coloured eyes darted around him, searching. The low encircling hills gave no clues.

There had to be a sign, he told himself.

For the briefest of moments the bounty hunter paused. Then out of the corner of one eye he saw something upon the crest of the rolling hills to his left. He swung, drew a gun and screwed up his eyes.

There was nothing there. He returned his gun to his belt.

Had he imagined it? Iron Eyes ran fingers through his long sweat-soaked hair. He was confused.

The shimmering heat haze was like looking into a pool of restless water. Nothing was exactly where his eyes said it was.

Pain cut through his skeletal body once more. He coughed and tasted the acrid flavour of blood. He spat and ran a sleeve across his mouth.

'I know ya out there someplace,' Iron Eyes snarled. 'I ain't loco. I seen ya.'

Then he felt the branding-irons thrust into his busted ribs again. He touched his side with thin

34

fingertips and winced. Looking down at his torn shirt he saw fresh blood seeping through the bandages which encircled him. He gritted his teeth and snorted through his flared nostrils like a raging bull.

Was pain conspiring with the rising heat to trick the bounty hunter? The question raced through his mind. He started to think that the aged sheriff back at Rio Valdo might have been correct when he had advised him to remain in town for a few days until his injuries started to mend.

His narrowed eyes returned to where he had thought he had seen a horseman for the briefest of moments seconds earlier. For what felt like an eternity he just stood and stared out at the distant rise.

Then a mere wisp of dust floated up into the blue morning sky from beyond the hilltop. It was the dust kicked up from the outlaw's horse's hoofs.

'Gotcha.' Iron Eyes spat blood again.

Every sinew in his injured frame knew that he had not been imagining it. He had caught a fleeting glimpse of his elusive prey.

A cruel smile covered his face. Iron Eyes pushed his left boot back into his stirrup again and grabbed hold of the saddle horn. He pulled himself atop the tired Indian pony and gathered the reins into his hands.

Again he spurred.

Again the pony responded.

THREE

With no thought for the condition of his already exhausted mount, Iron Eyes feverishly whipped the long tails of his reins across its shoulders and drove on across the parched landscape and then up the hill to where he had spotted the dust floating up into the heavens.

Again attempting to outrun the pain its master kept inflicting upon it, the pony somehow found a pace which was far beyond its capabilities.

It needed rest. It needed water. It needed food.

But Iron Eyes did not think of any of these things as he drove on. Racked by his own pain, all the bounty hunter could think of was Brewster. Iron Eyes knew the outlaw was so close he could smell his fear.

'C'mon!' Iron Eyes yelled out as he stabbed his spurs into the flesh of the spent creature beneath him. 'Run, damn it. We almost got the bastard.'

Driven by fear of the razor-sharp spurs, the pitiful

animal tried to achieve the impossible. Yet the pony could no longer keep up the pace demanded by its merciless master. The pathetic animal gave out a chilling noise then dropped suddenly to its knees. White foam came from its mouth. It began to slide back down the hill. Iron Eyes clung on to the reins and kept his boots firmly rammed into the stirrups as his mount continued to slide helplessly.

Only when the animal fell on to its side, did the long-legged man jump away from the pony. Iron Eyes managed to remain upright even though his boots could find no grip on the dusty hillside.

He watched the pony roll over helplessly several times as every ounce of its stamina evaporated from its malnourished body.

It did not stop its brutal descent until it reached the flat sun-bleached range. There was a sound that filled the ears of the bounty hunter as he carefully made his way back down toward his stricken mount.

It was the stomach churning noise only dying creatures made when death was closing on them.

With gritted teeth, Iron Eyes sighed heavily and glared at his pony. Most riders knew that it was wise to feed and water horses if you expected them to keep going mile after endless mile. But Iron Eyes had never regarded his mounts as anything but things you used to get to where you were going.

He was filled with a mixture of disgust and anger. Not with himself but the pony which had let him down.

'Ya just like all the others,' Iron Eyes growled loudly as the pony looked up at him with wide eyes. 'I hate horses. They always let ya down when the going gets tough.'

Iron Eyes could not understand how he seemed to be capable of surviving without hardly ever eating. He also could not quite work out why most creatures required water when he had always found hard liquor far more sustaining.

He kicked the pony venomously.

'Get up.'

It did not move.

Reluctantly the gaunt man plucked his four canteens from the sand where they had been strewn when the pony had hit the level ground. He raised each of the canteens in turn and shook them. One had water remaining in it whilst the others were empty. Iron Eyes tossed the empty canteens aside and then walked with the one which was half-full to the pony's head. He stepped over the creatures neck and unscrewed the stopper of the canteen. He stared down at the pony and began to pour the water over its open mouth. Most spilled over the sand but some found its target. Iron Eyes returned the stopper to the neck of the canteen and began to turn it. His eyes watched the animal as if a miracle might occur but it was too little too late.

The pony remained on the ground.

Angrily, Iron Eyes turned and made his way back

to where his saddle-bags lay half-covered by the pony.

One of the satchels was under the animal's hindquarters, whilst its twin was close to the mount's black tail. Iron Eyes went to bend down when he felt the sharp pain cut into his flesh again. He winced but continued to reach down for the weathered and worn leather bags that contained his entire wealth. One satchel was filled with the £3,000 reward money which he had received before leaving Rio Valdo. The other held two bottles of good whiskey.

Dropping the canteen beside him, Iron Eyes was forced to kneel before he could get hold of the bag with both hands. He pushed at the satchel and could feel the bounty money inside it. It was a mixture of paper and coins. But as he started to drag at the bag, he did not even think about the small fortune within his grasp. All he could think about was the two bottles of whiskey beneath the pony.

'Ya better not have busted them bottles, hoss,' Iron Eyes snarled at the animal who was incapable of moving.

Feverishly his bony hands scooped sand away until he found the other bag. To his horror it was damp. Damp with precious liquor. Fumes rose over the kneeling man. Mustering all his strength Iron Eyes pulled the bag free of the pony and then raised his hands to his nostrils. The scent of good whiskey filled him.

'Damn it all, hoss.' Iron Eyes cursed as his fingers unbuckled the satchel. He shook the contents on to the sand and stared in dismay. Broken glass and amber liquid spilled out. Both bottles had been crushed by the impact. 'Ya stupid lump of glue. Ya broke my liquor. Ya gonna pay for that.'

Iron Eyes stood up. He kicked at the pony again. It did not move or make a sound. He snorted and pulled one of his Navy Colts from his belt. He cocked its hammer, aimed at the head of the stricken Indian pony and then squeezed its trigger. A white flash spewed from the long, blue metal barrel. The pony shook as the lead ball crushed its skull.

The deafening sound echoed off the surrounding hills all around. Without a trace of emotion, Iron Eyes blew down the barrel of the .36 and then pushed the weapon back into his belt beside its twin.

'That'll teach ya.'

It was an unnamed creek in an unnamed valley and it led to the mighty yet distant Rio Grande. It was a place where soft fertile soil set between two thirty-mile-long stretches of sand-coloured rock walls had proved to be more valuable than gold itself. For this was an oasis in an otherwise arid country. For ten years this had been part of the empire belonging to powerful Don Miguel Sanchez. Sanchez was a Spanish nobleman who had come to Mexico in a brief lull between revolutions and used his fortune to create another one ten times bigger.

Sanchez was well-educated and fluent in four languages, which he had used to his advantage for most of his forty-two years of existence. An expert swordsman and shot, Sanchez had proved himself a true leader of men.

With an army of well-paid vaqueros he had used the vast valley to fatten up his cattle to sell to the Texas ranchers. They in turn would make thousands on the deals by reselling the beef on the hoof to the lucrative Eastern cattle buyers. For a decade everyone had prospered. None more so than Sanchez himself.

Sanchez had built his hacienda at the southernmost point of the valley where the rocks began. The massive whitewashed building stood in grounds of more than twenty acres. Resembling a small castle, the high-walled fortress had stables for fifty horses as well as quarters for his vaqueros and their families. At its core was a house for Don Miguel Sanchez and his family.

Few if any military structures in Mexico could equal the Sanchez hacienda for either size or quality. The empire which Sanchez had built for himself was just remote enough from the Mexican government. It was a country unto itself. It had its own laws and rituals which had nothing to do with the outside world.

Yet for the first time, the valley was under threat.

Not from armies but from a smaller, less noticeable enemy. For places like the unnamed valley and its sweet-water creek could not be kept a secret forever. Its sheer fertility had started to draw those who craved to eat something better than the dust which they had become accustomed to in the rest of the borderland. Families both American and Mexican had arrived secretly and set up small farms within the lush terrain.

With a milk cow, some hens, a little trapping of game and a small vegetable garden they too could enjoy a small taste of paradise. For nearly a year the dozen settlers had gone unnoticed by Sanchez. For even with thousands of steers grazing along the length of the thirty-mile valley there was still more than a third of the lush land remaining untouched and unused. It was in this part of the valley that the homesteaders had grouped themselves together. Their small cabins were virtually impossible to see from the creek that ran through the middle of the wide valley.

Set deep in the woods close to the foot of the tall stone rockface the settlers' arrival had gone totally unnoticed until the weather had briefly changed for the worse. The smoke of the settlers' chimneys had been spotted by some of the vaqueros and the news taken back to Sanchez.

Men like Don Miguel Sanchez protected what they regarded as theirs by any means they liked. Trespassing on land which the noble Spaniard regarded as his alone brought a swift, brutal and bloody response.

For there was no law in this remote land.

Only the law of Sanchez's own creation.

Like a medieval monarch Don Miguel Sanchez was judge, jury and executioner within the confines of his own vast kingdom. He bowed to no other authority than the one he had bestowed upon himself.

During the previous month one cabin after another had been discovered and then burned to the ground until there were only three left standing. Those who had occupied the destroyed cabins had either been killed or simply fled for fear of what Sanchez would do next. The last few cabins merely existed because they had not yet been discovered by the vaqueros.

The three remaining cabins were set roughly a quarter of a mile apart. One twenty-foot-square structure built with tree-trunks was occupied by more than eight souls from the parched Mexican heartland. Jose Garcia and his beloved wife Maria were peasants who had struggled to feed their six children until they had joined the inflow of settlers into the valley. Now for the first time in their lives they were able to feed their offspring and themselves.

Another was the home of the James family. Stan James was only in his forties yet looked at least ten years older. Hard toil had taken its toll upon the man who claimed to be from Scotland and yet sounded as though he hailed from Kentucky. His wife was a small woman named Olive whose white hair belied her thirty-two years. They had two daughters who were five and eight years of age.

Both Garcia and James had wanted to pack up their wagons and follow the survivors out of the valley when the burning and killing had started. But they had been stopped by the encouraging words of their neighbour Dan Landon.

Landon was six feet in height and as strong as an ox. He and his wife Wilma had arrived first in the valley with their seven year old son Billy. Landon was a man who knew how to wield an axe, and had built practically all of the settlers' cabins himself. Unlike the others who had followed his lead and entered the fertile valley, Landon had not feared the reputation of Don Miguel Sanchez.

He had a blind faith that this place was where he was meant to be. No man, however powerful he might be, would ever frighten him off what he regarded as his own small piece of happiness.

He had found the garden of Eden.

No snake in human form was going to trick or spook him into leaving without a fight. Yet Landon was no fool. He knew that danger was looming with every passing day as Sanchez's vaqueros continued their search for more trespassers. Each day the well-armed riders had come closer. It was only a matter of time before the vaqueros found what they were seeking.

Landon wanted to fight but knew that the lives of many innocents were dependent upon him. The children of the three remaining families were defenceless. Even with a body packed with powerful muscles, as his was, Landon was wise enough to know that a single bullet could end his days.

Apart from his strength and courage, Landon only had a squirrel gun to defend so many. It was not enough. Knowing the vaqueros were getting even closer as their search widened, he had ordered that neither James not Gracia should allow their women to light their fires to cook. All meals had to be cold until the danger passed. If it ever passed.

The smoke had brought death and only luck had saved them from the same fate as the other settlers.

There was a time when caution was the safest option.

Landon and his neighbours had to be vigilant.

The only other option was to die.

FOUR

If the Devil had ever designed a landscape to suit his every need, it would have been the one in which the infamous Iron Eyes had found himself trapped. If there had ever been any grass across the rolling range and hillsides it had been burned to the root long ago by the ceaseless beating down of the unrelenting sun. It was hotter than hell and there was no shade. The thin, injured figure had somehow defied his own severe pain and the wound which refused to stop bleeding and had vainly tried to find the tracks of the outlaw he sought.

The blood had already soaked him in its own brutal shade of crimson but Iron Eyes stubbornly staggered on. It was as though there was more blood on his ragged clothing than remained flowing through his veins. Iron Eyes had left his saddle strapped to the dead pony and taken only the canteen and saddle-bags with him on his quest. But even these were beginning to weigh him down as he forced one foot ahead of another to keep moving forward.

He had cleared the first hill easily but now his strength was beginning to ebb. He held his hand over the broken ribs which had poked through the catgut stitches and the bandages and kept on. The sound of the remaining drops of water inside the canteen blended with the noise of his bloodstained spurs. Even though he still had a half-pint of water remaining, Iron Eyes felt no desire to consume it. The fumes from the saddle-bag satchel over his wide shoulder was enough to fuel his appetite for the time being.

Shadows swept steadily across the ground ahead of him. He glanced up and saw the wide wing-spans of the vultures, which were either interested in the corpse of the pony or the exhausted figure of its sweat-soaked master.

Iron Eyes tried to lick his cracked lips but there was no spittle. He inhaled the whiskey fumes deep and thought about the amber liquor he craved.

He knew that there just had to be some hard liquor ahead of him some place. Wherever more than a few men gathered together for any length of time, one of them would manage to make something resembling whiskey. All he had to do was find some men and he would also find something worth quenching his thirst with. He had enough money in his bags to buy an ocean of whiskey and would willingly have exchanged it all for a bottle.

47

He looked around him. The heat haze was sickening. It rippled the very air itself. It masked everything further than twenty yards away from his sand-caked eyes.

Then a sound caught his attention. He reached the top of the hill, paused, blinked hard and listened. He recognized the sound of fast-flowing water.

The sun was high overhead and beat down mercilessly. Iron Eyes studied the parched landscape towards where the sun danced upon the creek's waters. Most travellers might have noticed the marked difference in the scenery that he observed from that which had tortured him for so many endless miles. But Iron Eyes only saw a place where he might be able to find another horse. And another bottle.

He rubbed his cracked lips across the sleeve of his free arm and sighed heavily. Every breath was now a nightmare. It was like being skewered by a butcher's rod.

Once more Iron Eyes defied his pain and began to make his way down the hillside towards the creek.

To his left trees and lush undergrowth fed off the fast-flowing water which ran through the valley but this meant nothing to the bounty hunter who carefully edged his way down the sun-burned hillside.

His attention was on the ground before him. His eyes searched for the hoof tracks of which he had

48

somehow lost sight a few miles back. This ground was rougher than any he had ever tracked across before. Sand and millions of small sharp stones gave no clues as to where Joe Brewster had gone. An army could have ridden across this ground without leaving a trace.

Iron Eyes knew that if he had not been wounded he would never have lost sight of the hoof tracks. But he was wounded and his renowned hunting skills had deserted him.

After what felt like a lifetime, Iron Eyes reached the level ground and paused. He pulled his blood-soaked trail-coat away from his skeletal frame and looked down at the broken tips of ribs which protruded from the bandages. Everything was soaked in red yet the bounty hunter felt no alarm. He had seen far worse in his days.

Then the sound of the water drew his attention again.

Iron Eyes lifted his chin and stared at the glistening shallow water which flowed from the valley out into the harsher land to his right.

Most men in his condition would have looked at the water with joy in their souls. They would have drunk their fill and said prayers of thanks, but not the emaciated figure. All Iron Eyes could see was an obstacle.

'Damn it all!' he cursed. He screwed up his eyes against the bright reflection of the overhead sun, which dazzled him.

Iron Eyes pulled the guns from his pants belt and looked at them. The blood had covered both Navy Colts. He staggered unsteadily to the water's edge and forced himself to kneel down. He carefully washed the blood from the blue steel weapons and dropped them into the deep pocket of his trail-coat. The sound of the loose bullets filled his ears as the guns found the bottom of the deep pocket. He scooped water into the cupped palms of his hands and splashed it over his head several times. The cold liquid felt fine. He then splashed more over the bandages. It did not help or ease the pain. Then he looked around him, trying to work out where he ought to head from here.

To his left there was a lush valley shielded from the searing rays of the sun by the high sand-coloured rock walls. To his right there was nothing but more of the same type of arid terrain of which he had already had his bellyful.

The choice was simple.

He gave another deep sigh. A troublesome thought occurred to Iron Eyes. He seemed to be having trouble filling his lungs since he had set out on this long trek. His fingers pushed the ribs back into his pitifully thin frame again. He winced.

'I need strapping up tighter than ever,' he muttered to himself before forcing his weary frame up off the ground. This time he did not reach his full height. It was as though someone was standing upon his shoulders.

Someone damned heavy.

He looked up to where the green vegetation started. There were an awful lot of trees there, he told himself. Trees gave shade. He glanced at his hands. The skin was blistered by the unceasing rays of the sun. He ran the fingers of his right hand through his long hair.

It was wet with sweat and creek water. He shook his head like a hound dog after stepping in from the rain.

'Reckon there might just be someone up yonder with a horse I can buy,' Iron Eyes said as he began to walk towards the fertile valley. 'Or steal.'

For the first time in a long time, Iron Eyes felt the sharp drop in temperature as he staggered beneath the shade of a huge well-nourished tree close to the water's edge. It felt good.

He had ventured less than a mile into the cool wood when he heard something which managed to cut through his weariness. It was a familiar sound. It was the sound of a snorting, galloping horse being ridden on the other side of the creek.

Iron Eyes pushed through the brush between the tree-trunks until he had an uninterrupted view of the fast-flowing water and beyond. He pressed a hand against the rough bark of the nearest tree and rested against it.

He could hear the rider and horse approaching but could not see them. Iron Eyes shook his head. His mind filled with images of all the Apaches he had confronted over the years. They had seemed to dislike him even more than he hated them. Again he pushed his ribs back inside his flesh.

Could this place be filled with Indians?

The thought chilled him to the bone. He knew that he was not fighting fit. There was no chance he would win an encounter with Indians. A bead of sweat trailed down his scarred features and dripped from his chin.

Iron Eyes gritted his sharp teeth. His bony fingers went to his shirt. They searched and then found what they were looking for. He pulled a thin cigar remnant from his shirt pocket. It was twisted and stained with blood, but he did not care. He pushed it between his teeth and then found a match and ran a thumbnail across it.

He raised its flame to the end of the cigar and dragged in the smoke as deep as it would go. He closed his eyes for a few seconds and then allowed the smoke to drift from his lips. He tossed the match into the creek, screwed up his eyes and focused across the water.

Instinctively his right hand pulled one of his Navy Colts from his coat pocket. His thumb dragged back the gun's hammer until it locked fully into position.

Iron Eyes leaned against the tree and held the gun at hip level. He strained to hear. He closed his eyes and tried to picture what his ears were telling him.

'Think!' he snarled at himself.

It was a single rider, his ears told him.

He nodded to himself. It was also a big horse. It was not a small agile pony.

Whoever was riding along the valley, it was no Indian.

'C'mon, pard,' Iron Eyes whispered through a cloud of acrid smoke. 'I'm ready for ya.'

FIVE

To the relief of the weary bounty hunter the approaching horseman was indeed alone, as he had suspected. The vaquero had ridden thirty miles to this place. Twenty with his fellow vaqueros in search of more trespassers within the domain of Don Miguel Sanchez. The others had parted company with Sanchez's top vaquero more than ten miles back and were scouring the dense fertile land to either side of the creek whilst the solitary rider had made his way to the very end of the unnamed valley.

Pedro Ruiz was a proud, confident man who thought a lot of himself and little of others. It was a trait which would soon send him on a journey to purgatory.

Iron Eyes squinted through the bright sunlight across the dazzling water at the rider who sat astride his tall palomino stallion. The weary bounty hunter did not yet know that he was one of the many vaqueros who worked for Don Miguel Sanchez and

54

had been sent out on a deadly mission to hunt down and kill all those who had strayed into the valley.

Without ever questioning his master, Ruiz had willingly carried out his deadly instructions many times since he had started working for the mysterious Sanchez. Even amongst his fellow vaqueros, Ruiz was regarded as the most brutal and deadly of them all.

Yet Ruiz had never encountered anyone like the man who secretly watched his every move. Iron Eyes gripped his gun firmly in his hand and studied the well-dressed rider carefully. He saw nothing to be afraid of. He had encountered many vaqueros over the years he had ridden along the border. But none had been quite as well-adorned as this one. The black sombrero with its silver stitching was perched upon his head with only its colourful drawstring preventing it from falling on to the back of the blue, well-tailored jacket.

For all his finery, Ruiz aroused no fear in the onlooker.

The vaquero's ivory gun-grip gleamed in the sunlight as Ruiz drew rein and stopped his mount.

Iron Eyes had never had any trouble with vaqueros and did not imagine that this one would be any different. He relaxed and lowered his Navy Colt before stepping out from the cover of the trees and undergrowth. The lean figure saw nothing to be afraid of in this fancy horseman. Iron Eyes

staggered out into the open towards the the creek.
He began walking towards Ruiz through the shallow
fast-moving water.

It was a mistake.

'Hey!' Iron Eyes called out above the sound of
flowing water. 'Ya speak American, amigo?'

The Mexican swung around on his saddle and
glared at the brutalized vision which approached.
Ruiz's eyes widened. The blood-soaked man who
had started to wade through the creek was unlike
anything he had ever set eyes upon before. Not
even in his worst nightmares had he seen such an
apparition. With the long mane of black hair
hanging limply over his scarred face Iron Eyes
looked even more fearsome than normal. The
startled Ruiz steadied his stallion and in one swift,
well-oiled movement pulled the gun from its ornate
holster. Then a torrent of words flew back at Iron
Eyes in a tongue the wounded man recognized but
could not understand.

The hunter of men stopped.

His eyes burned at the man's hand and the gun it
had drawn clear of the holster.

Then, to his utter surprise, Iron Eyes saw the gun
being raised and levelled at him. His keen eyesight
focused on the thumb as it started to pull back the
hammer.

'I wouldn't do that if I was you!' the bounty
hunter warned the vaquero loudly.

The sound of the hammer clicking filled his ears.

Now there was no more time for words.

There would be no more warnings.

Iron Eyes swung his arm upward. His index finger squeezed the Navy Colt's trigger at the same moment as the horseman duplicated the action.

Two deafening blasts. Two spirited bullets cut across the creek water in both directions.

Iron Eyes felt the heat of the lead ball as it passed within inches of his ear. His long hair kicked up as the red-hot bullet lifted the side of his long, damp mane.

Then he narrowed his eyes. His thumb dragged the hammer back again. He was about to fire once more but there was no call. Iron Eyes watched the stallion spin around as its master was jerked violently backwards. A trail of blood droplets flew into the morning air like crimson petals. The high cantle of the saddle had prevented the vaquero from being knocked backwards from his high perch but the bounty hunter knew his aim had somehow been deadly.

Now the magnificent palomino had a corpse for a rider.

The tall skeletal figure waded through the water towards the horse and its lifeless cargo. The horse was terrified of what it saw and smelled. For the memories of death hung on every inch of the bounty hunter. The stallion flared its nostrils. It went to rear up but Iron Eyes was too close. His bony hand grabbed at its reins and held the palomino in check.

It took every scrap of his dwindling energy but the bounty hunter would not allow a mere horse, however big it was, to defeat him.

After a few moments the animal was subdued and stopped its fighting. Iron Eyes held on to the reins and then staggered a couple of steps to the leg of the dead vaquero propped between the horn and cantle of the well crafted saddle. Iron Eyes pulled the rider's boot from the nearest stirrup and then heaved the leg upward. He watched as the body tumbled off the back of the stallion.

The Mexican landed on the damp soil like a rag doll.

'It don't pay to shoot at Iron Eyes, boy.' The words were spat at the body with bitter contempt. He had no idea why the rider had decided to shoot at him and really did not care. It had proved profitable.

Now the blood-soaked bounty hunter had a new horse. He had attained half of what he desired. Iron Eyes dropped his gun back into the deep trail-coat pocket and then used his fingers to release the bags from behind the saddle. He pulled them towards him and heard the sound of liquid in one of its satchels.

A smile etched across the face of the half-dead man.

He quickly unbuckled the swollen bag, pushed his bony hand inside and then found the thing he desired. He pulled the bottle of pale-yellow mezcal free and stared at it.

'Well, it ain't whiskey but it's liquor and that's all that counts,' Iron Eyes said as he studied it. 'If Mexicans can drink this stuff, then so can I.'

It was two-thirds full and had a worm in it.

'Damn it all,' Iron Eyes muttered to himself wryly. 'Why'd these heathen varmints wanna put a bug in good liquor for? Still, I reckon my belly could use a little grub.'

He yanked the cork with his teeth and spat it away. He would not need it again. Iron Eyes lifted the bottle and placed its neck to his cracked lips. He started to drink and did not stop until there were only fumes remaining inside the clear glass. Even the worm was consumed.

Iron Eyes threw the bottle away and searched the rest of the vaquero's bags more thoroughly. He pulled out a box of small black cigars and filled his pockets with them. Then he pulled his own saddle-bags off his bony shoulder and tossed them across the neck of the palomino.

Gripping the saddle horn he raised his left leg until his boot toe found the stirrup. The mezcal had given him renewed strength. He pulled himself up on to the saddle and then swung the horse around.

The palomino tried to fight but it was useless.

The bounty hunter had never possessed such a huge mount before, let alone ridden one. It must have been twice the size of the ponies he was used

59

to riding. He sat in the bloody saddle and looked all around him silently. Iron Eyes had never been so high off the ground before when mounted. It was an experience he liked. He could not believe how far he was able to see from his high vantage point.

'Reckon I better look after you a tad better than I done with my last few animals,' Iron Eyes said to the mighty stallion beneath him. 'Ya could be worth ya weight in gold if'n ya can run as fast as them muscles of yours say.'

Again he looked down at the ribs which poked out from his flesh. There was no hiding from the fact that it was a severe injury.

But Iron Eyes ignored it. He placed one of the new cigars between his lips and struck a match across the saddle horn. He inhaled the smoke and let it linger in his lungs for a while before blowing it at the sky. Between the liquor and the cigar smoke, the pain seemed to ease.

'Reckon we oughta go take us a look upstream, boy,' Iron Eyes told the horse through a cloud of grey smoke.

With a skill to equal any vaquero, Iron Eyes expertly turned the stallion and aimed its nose at the valley, where he imagined he might find someone who could tend his busted ribs and stop his bleeding.

It was time to show the powerful creature he sat astride who was the boss.

He thrust his spurs into the flesh of the palomino

hard and held on to the reins firmly. The animal gave out a stunned whinny of protest. Ruiz had never drawn the blood of his noble steed but Iron Eyes had already done so. The horse suddenly realized that not all riders were the same.

Desperately the stallion tried to unseat the bounty hunter by rearing up and kicking out at the air but Iron Eyes was not to be bucked. The high cantle and saddle horn held the thin figure firmly between them. In the end the stallion understood it would never defeat this ghostly horseman. It gave up the fight. Iron Eyes steadied the stallion, then dragged the reins hard to his right before driving his sharp spurs into the palomino once again. This time the animal obeyed its new owner and thundered away from the corpse which only minutes earlier had been its master.

Now it had a new master.

The wide-eyed creature had already learned the difference.

SIX

It was dusk and the large man knew that total darkness would come within the hour not only to his but also his neighbours small dirt farms. Yet as Dan Landon moved between the trees a few dozen yards from his well-hidden cabin the memory of the two gunshots he had heard on the afternoon air remained branded into his troubled mind. It had been almost a month since he had heard gunfire and that had brought death to the majority of the other settlers along the valley. Landon rested his muscular right shoulder against a tree-trunk and stared out into the dense woods as the sun's last rays filtered through the tree canopies.

The wood was his family's only shield from the forces of evil which he knew might return at any time. The thought chilled his mighty frame.

The sound of two shots had stopped the songbirds that afternoon. Landon wondered what else had been silenced, away in the distance.

Who had fired those shots? he asked himself.

Had it been the vaqueros?

The question had haunted Landon for hours although he had not mentioned a word of his concern either to his wife or to his young son. Every sinew in his body told him that if it had been the vaqueros they must have found new prey further along the valley. He knew that his neighbours were safe as their small farms were in the opposite direction from where the shots had emanated.

But Landon was also well aware that the long valley could play tricks to a man's senses. He knew that the trees and high rock walls to either side of the creek had a way of twisting sounds. Some called it echoes but Landon had another word for it.

Trickery.

He had read his Bible many times and knew that if this was a kind of Eden, then there had to be many serpents within its vast confines. Not the sidewinder variety but the two-legged sort who would do anything to trick the few remaining families who had not yet been driven out.

Perhaps the man known as Sanchez had instructed his men to try and frighten those they could not catch. Firing blind shots could cause game to flee from their hiding-places and be trapped and killed. The same might be said of men. They could be scared out into the open and into the gun sights of those who hunted them.

Landon had never required a gun like so many of

his age in the West. He had never even learned how to use one, but since he had brought his wife and child to this place he wished he had something with which he could keep the vaqueros at bay.

He looked down at his powerful arms.

No shirt had ever been able to contain them without bursting stitches. The low sun was now behind the high rock walls and an eerie glow filled the valley all around him.

He sighed.

Landon had seen the strange eerie light many times in the last year but it had never troubled him before. This was one night when he actually feared the coming of darkness.

Who was it who had fired those two shots?

And why?

A thousand answers sped their way through his mind. None of them made any sense. For he had no way of knowing for sure who or why those two shots had been unleashed.

But he wanted to know.

He wanted to know so badly his guts hurt.

Perhaps the vaqueros had decided to try something different this time in their quest to track down the people who trespassed in the beautiful fertile valley, Landon told himself.

Maybe they had ridden to the very end of the valley where the desert started and were now sweeping the woods to both sides of the creek in one last attempt to find the last of the settlers and destroy them.

Dan Landon raised both his large hands and rubbed his eyes in a vain effort to wipe his fear away with the sweat. Again he inhaled deeply and tried to remain strong.

Then he heard something some yards away from where he stood beside the tree.

It was the breaking of twigs.

Then he heard the sound of a horse snorting.

There was no mistaking what it was. A rider was headed straight towards him and his cabin, he told himself silently. His heart began to race.

The big man moved behind the tree and attempted to hide his muscular form from the eyes of whoever it was who was coming towards him.

He swallowed hard.

His ears could hear the horse moving through the brush. It was getting louder and closer with every beat of his pounding heart. Was it the vaqueros?

Now he really wished that he had a gun.

Landon bit his lower lip. He needed a weapon, he told himself. Something. Anything. He turned and ran back towards the cabin and the axe he had left in the stump of a tree hours earlier.

He pulled the axe free and then rushed to the open door of his cabin.

'Stay inside, Wilma,' Landon whispered to his wife. 'Keep little Billy quiet. And lock it.'

The woman moved to the door. Her concern

showed. 'What's wrong, Dan? What's wrong?'

He patted her arm. 'I don't know but I'm gonna find out.'

She was about to speak again but her husband was gone. He ran back to where he had heard the rider.

Wilma closed and bolted the door.

'What's wrong, Ma?' the boy asked.

'Be quiet, Billy,' she implored her son. 'Be as quiet as you can.'

Dan Landon held the long-handled axe in his hands. It was a hefty tool which he prayed he would not have to turn into a weapon. For men like Landon could chop trees down but he wondered whether he could ever do the same to another man.

Could he? The question bore into his mind. His eyes glanced back at the well-hidden cabin and his thoughts were for the two people inside it.

He had his answer.

Dan Landon knew that he could and would do anything to protect them.

He knelt behind the tree trunk and began to pray.

For what felt like several lifetimes, Landon waited. His large hands gripped the handle of the axe as he listened to the horse getting closer.

Then he saw the bushes ahead of him part.

The dim light hung around the horse and its rider as they pushed out into the small clearing between the trees.

Landon leapt to his feet and stepped away from the tree. He raised the axe and then focused his eyes.

'Sweet lord!' he gasped in stunned horror.

SEVEN

Men like Dan Landon did not feel fear in the same way that most men did, but the horrific monstrosity which came silently through the bushes chilled him to the bone. It was as if his own worst nightmares had suddenly taken shape and were coming from the very depths of his imagination and manifesting into reality.

Every fibre in Landon's body wanted to turn and run but he knew that it was impossible. He was unable to move as his eyes focused on the hideous apparition.

For the horseman was not one of the deadly vaqueros he had expected. In fact he looked barely human. The rider was drenched in blood and covered in trail dust. He had slumped over the neck of the large palomino stallion but the high horn and cantle of the Mexican saddle had refused to allow him to fall from his lofty perch.

It was impossible for Landon to tell whether Iron Eyes was asleep or unconscious. The ghostlike figure just swayed like a lifeless shadow.

Landon felt his own sweat trace down his spine as the horse stopped before him. The dirt farmer held on to the bridle and looked hard up at the face of the bounty hunter hidden by the long limp strands of hair. The light was almost gone but there was enough of it left to make the hair on the nape of Landon's neck rise.

He had seen many things in his time but he had never seen anything like the scarred features of Iron Eyes. Landon was scared to death.

The long limp black hair was something Landon had only previously seen on Apaches, but this was no Indian.

Unsure whether the bounty hunter was alive or dead, Landon cautiously ventured to the saddle and the man's lean blood-soaked leg. His eyes studied the rider. It appeared that there was very little of this pitiful soul not drenched in blood.

Landon raised a finger and jabbed it into the leg.

'You alive, stranger?' he managed to ask fearfully.

It seemed a stupid question, even to the man who had uttered it. His mind told him that nobody who had lost that amount of blood could possibly be anything but dead. Landon peeled the side of the trail-coat away from the bounty hunter's body. He stared at the bony frame revealed beneath the shredded shirt.

If this man was breathing, Landon certainly could not detect any hint of it.

Landon went to release the coat when he saw the sharp busted rib bones poking out from what had once been bandages. He gritted his teeth. He could almost feel the horseman's pain.

'Mister?' he questioned again.

Iron Eyes still did not move.

Dan Landon dropped his axe. He pulled the spurred boot from the stirrup and took the weight of the emaciated figure in his massive arms. He gently pulled Iron Eyes free of the horse and then turned towards his cabin.

He had taken only one step when he realized that this tall figure weighed less than his own wife.

'I don't know who you were, friend,' Landon said as he began to walk. 'But I'll bury you and read from the Good Book over your bones.'

Suddenly without warning or sound Landon felt something as cold as ice pushed under his square jaw. He stopped walking when he heard the hammer of the Navy Colt being cocked.

'I'd rather ya didn't bury me just yet,' Iron Eyes whispered in a low drawl.

'You ain't dead?' Landon's voice was confused.

Iron Eyes forced a defiant smile at the face close to his own. 'Now that's a matter of opinion that a lotta folks can't agree on. Some folks reckon I died a long time back but it ain't smart to listen to that sort of locobean.'

'You're alive!' Landon gulped.

'Don't sound so disappointed.' Iron Eyes

coughed. 'There's still time.'

Landon went to lower the lightweight to the ground when Iron Eyes pushed the barrel of his gun up into the throat of the farmer even harder.

'Take me to that tree stump over yonder. My legs are a tad tired.'

'OK. OK. Don't shoot.' The muscular man did as he was told and carried his bloody cargo to the tree stump close to the front of the cabin. He gently lowered the injured man down until Iron Eyes was seated on the stump. 'Please don't shoot me. I got me a wife and boy in there.'

Iron Eyes released the hammer slowly and then dropped the gun back into his trail-coat pocket.

'I wasn't gonna shoot you, friend,' he admitted.

'Then why'd you ram that pistol in my neck?' Landon growled loudly.

'I didn't want ya to drop me.' The bounty hunter sighed. 'I don't figure this old body of mine could take being dropped at the moment.'

Landon marched to the stallion and led it to his cabin and the unexpected guest, who watched his every move through the long sweat-soaked hair. As he reached the bounty hunter he paused and studied the mount and its livery.

'Ain't this a strange rig for a man like you to have on a horse?'

Iron Eyes nodded in agreement. 'I killed a vaquero downstream to get that nag. Best bullet I ever wasted.'

Landon smiled. 'You killed one of Sanchez's vaqueros?'

'Yep.'

'Then you just made yourself a friend for life!' Landon explained. 'There's bin a whole bunch of vaqueros killing and burning us settlers for the past month or so.'

Iron Eyes studied the man. 'How come?'

Landon shrugged. 'It's all to do with a varmint named Sanchez. He figures he owns this valley and everything in it, and he don't cotton to trespassers. He runs a small army of vaqueros to do his bidding and they sure relish doing it.'

The bounty hunter pulled a cigar from his pocket and pushed it between his lips. He scratched a match across his pants leg and then inhaled the smoke. His eyes narrowed as he blew the flame from the blackened match. Suddenly he began to understand why the Mexican had opened up on him.

'How many of you trespassers are there?'

'Only three of us left, but we all got family.'

'Ya got guns to protect them families?'

'Nope.'

It was a thoughtful Iron Eyes who brooded for a while as smoke trailed from his mouth. He nodded as if answering a question only he had heard before looking back up at the young man.

'Reckon ya might need a little help by the sounds of it.'

Landon smiled, then reached out and knocked at the cabin door with his large clenched fist.

'Open up, Wilma honey. We got us a sick friend out here who needs tending.'

Iron Eyes looked down at his side. 'Ya right. I am in a sort of fix with these ribs of mine.'

'Did the vaquero do that?' Landon asked.

'Nope. An outlaw back at Rio Valdo got lucky.'

'Outlaw?'

'Yep.' Iron Eyes inhaled as much smoke as he could. 'I'm a bounty hunter and I'm on the trail of a dirty varmint called Joe Brewster. I'm gonna kill that bastard when I catch up with his stinking carcass.'

'Kill him?'

'Yep. That's what I do. I kill bad folks.'

The door opened and the small fragile female looked out at her husband. For a moment she did not see the crouched figure seated on the tree stump. When the bounty hunter turned his head she raised a hand to her mouth in shock.

Landon moved to her. 'Don't be feared, Wilma.'

The bounty hunter gripped the cigar in his teeth. 'The name's Iron Eyes, ma'am. I'm sorry to have frightened ya.'

She was trembling. 'My name's Wilma Landon. I'm Dan's woman, Mr Iron Eyes.'

Iron Eyes nodded slowly but he was looking past her dress at the small boy who was watching him intently from the cover of the doorway.

73

'And what they call you, young'un?'

The boy said nothing. He just kept watching the horrific figure beside his father.

'This is Billy, Iron Eyes.' Landon said proudly.

Somehow the thin man with the cigar gripped between his teeth managed to get to his feet and stumble towards the wide-eyed child. Billy Landon stood his ground even though he had never seen anyone like Iron Eyes before.

'I like ya, Billy,' Iron Eyes said. 'Ya don't waste time gabbing like us old 'uns. Ya listen and watch. That's the mark of a real man.'

Dan Landon stepped up close to the bounty hunter and supported him with his powerful arms.

'Come inside, Iron Eyes. I'll tend ya wounds and Wilma will rustle up some vittles for you.'

Wilma followed her man into the cabin. 'You think it's safe for me to light the fire so I can cook something hot, Dan?'

Dan helped the bounty hunter on to a cot.

'Light the fire, Wilma. I can't figure why but I ain't scared no more.'

EIGHT

There were eight of them. Eight riders who all bore the same allegiance to Don Miguel Sanchez that their fallen comrade Pedro Ruiz had shared. They, like the settlers they sought, had heard the brief salvo hours earlier when the sun had been high. The sound of two gunshots had lasted barely longer than the beat of a heart and yet their echoes had travelled ten miles along the unnamed valley's high-walled sides.

Each of the vaqueros in turn had been drawn by the invisible strings of curiosity away from the dense woods to either side of the creek and started their long ride together to the very end of the lush valley.

A million stars had replaced the blue sky long before the eight horsemen had managed to reach the place where the merciless desert lay, just beyond the mouth of the fertile valley. Even the dim light of the stars could not conceal the total dissimilarity between the two lands. Water sprayed up from the hoofs of the powerful mounts as their masters drove them through the shallow waters to where the sound of shooting had come from hours earlier. For a moment none of them could see anything untoward. Then the lead rider stood in his stirrups and eased back on his reins.

It was Pepe Gomez who had drawn rein when his black stallion had suddenly shied. The violent and abrupt refusal of the mount to go any further would have thrown most riders from their saddles, but not Gomez. The experienced vaquero steadied his spooked horse as his seven companions stopped around him.

Gomez balanced and looked just ahead of the line of riders at something on the wet soil just ahead of them.

There was an unnerving aroma hanging on the air and the eight horses had sensed it long before their masters. Each unnerved animal clawed at the ground with its hoofs and attempted to back away.

'What is wrong, Pepe?' one of the other horsemen asked.

Gomez held his powerful animal in check, then raised a long finger and pointed to what looked like a black log on the soil close to the edge of the creek.

'There!' Gomez said. 'See it, amigos?'

'It is just a log or something, Pepe.'

'Smell the air, my friend,' Gomez said knowingly. 'Logs do not smell of death.'

One of the vaqueros dropped from his saddle

and tossed his reins to Gomez.

'I will look,' he said.

The seven mounted men watched as the vaquero walked through the strange bluish starlight towards the black object. Then they saw him turn in disbelief.

'It is Pedro!' he gasped.

Gomez looked around the area and then back at his fellow riders. He sighed heavily.

'What are you looking for, Pepe?'

'Where is his horse?' Gomez asked curiously. 'Where is Pedro's magnificent horse? It would never leave him.'

All eight men searched the darkness for any sign of Pedro Ruiz's palomino.

There was none.

'Someone has killed Pedro and stolen his stallion,' another of the vaqueros said.

Gomez dismounted and walked to where Ruiz's body lay. He had never liked the vaquero and had secretly feared him for years but he still knew that there was an unwritten law that he and his men all lived and died by. When one of your own is killed, it was your duty to avenge your fallen comrade.

Gomez knelt and turned the body over until it lay on its back. The lifeless eyes were dull. The vaquero reached over and closed Ruiz's eyes with his long fingers. Gomez then looked at the body carefully. He wanted to discover how this ruthless man had met his death.

To his utter surprise he could see just one well-placed bullet hole.

The vaquero's gun was still in Ruiz's stiffening hand. Gomez pulled the gun free and opened its chamber to inspect the bullets in its cylinder. He knew that Don Miguel Sanchez's top gun always kept his weapon fully loaded. Only one brass casing showed that it had been struck by the firing-pin on the gun hammer. The five other bullets were untouched and intact.

'Pedro fired only one bullet, mi amigos,' he informed the other vaqueros.

Two more of the vaqueros dropped from their mounts and moved towards the kneeling man curiously.

'Are you sure Pedro fired only once?' one of them asked in amazement.

'How many bullets hit him, Pepe?' another vaquero queried.

Gomez looked at the approaching men. 'Just one. I think he was dead before he had a chance to fire again.'

Both vaqueros stopped.

'Was he shot in the back?'

Gomez rose up and shook his head. 'No, amigos. This was no ambush. Pedro had a showdown with someone and he lost. Whoever it was who shot him was either the luckiest of men or the most deadly shot I have ever seen.'

There was a stunned silence. None of them could

imagine who could have outdrawn Ruiz and used just one bullet to end his life. It seemed impossible. They had all seen Ruiz shoot the head off a chicken from the back of a galloping horse. Who could have bettered Pedro Ruiz?

Gomez studied the churned-up ground thoughtfully. He looked at the others and then pointed to the dense woodland to his right.

'Pedro's horse went that way.'

'What shall we do, Pepe? Should we follow?'

Gomez removed his sombrero and ran a hand through his sweat-soaked hair.

'Luis shall take Pedro's body back to the hacienda and inform Don Miguel of what has happened.' Gomez said firmly. 'The rest of us shall make camp here and when the sun rises again we shall follow the tracks to find and kill the murderer.'

'Who do you think did this, Pepe?'

Gomez returned his hat to his head and tightened its drawstring. His eyes cast across the faces of the seven others in turn.

'Only the Devil himself could have done this, amigos.'

NINE

Even darkness could not hide the massive whitewashed hacienda which Don Miguel Sanchez had erected as a monument and proof of his unparalleled power. It seemed to all who approached it to fill the very sky, looming over the southern end of the valley as a warning to anyone who dared enter the lands claimed by Sanchez.

Blazing torches were perched along its high walls and to either side of its well-fortified entrance. Their flickering light illuminated the trail which led to its solitary entrance.

Luis Fernandez had made good time back to the imposing edifice considering the weight of the lifeless body which was tied behind his high cantle. It had taken barely five hours to negotiate the long ride through the valley but every stride of his stallion had brought fear to the vaquero.

Fernandez slowed his mount and then called out across the darkness to the sentries who he knew would be guarding their leader and all those who dwelled behind the high walls. There were always at least half a dozen well-armed men on duty throughout the night.

The rider reined in and waited a hundred yards from the sturdy drawbridge until he heard the chains begin to lower the heavy wooden gangway to the ground.

Only when he saw two of the guards venture out and signal to him did Fernandez jab his spurs into the sides of the muscular stallion beneath him. The horse responded and rode across the clearing and over the wooden drawbridge. He had no sooner entered the courtyard than he heard the sturdy chains raising the drawbridge back up again.

The sound of hoofs on wood had echoed all around the area and alerted those within the hacienda that someone had arrived. He rode to the impressive tiled steps and pulled back on his reins. The stallion halted and snorted at the ground. For hours the thoroughbred animal had vainly attempted to outrun the smell of death it carried on its back.

'Don Miguel! Don Miguel!' Fernandez bellowed out below the tiled steps which led from the courtyard up to where Sanchez had his own private quarters. For a few moments the vaquero saw nothing above him. Then he saw light race across the glass of the windows as one lamp after another was lit.

Fernandez was nervous.

He had good reason.

Even though he had done nothing wrong, he knew the murderous proclivities of his leader. Those who brought bad news to Sanchez often paid with their lives. The vaquero dismounted as the guards surrounded his horse and the lifeless body tied across its saddle cantle. Then they all looked up at the fearsome man who was walking barefooted down the tiled steps towards them.

Don Miguel Sanchez was draped in the finest silk dressing-gown and held a cocked .45 in his left hand. He said nothing as he descended to the men and the horse.

There was a fire in the eyes of Sanchez. A fire which all who saw it knew would not be easily extinguished.

'What is this, you pathetic dog?' Don Miguel Sanchez shouted at the man who held on to the reins of the stallion. 'What have you done? Why is Pedro dead?'

Fernandez bowed fearfully.

'No, Don Miguel, we found the body of poor Pedro at the end of the valley. He was slain by someone, Don Miguel. Pepe told me to bring it to you. This I have done.'

Sanchez walked to the side of the stallion and signalled to one of his men to lift the head of the dead vaquero. The nearest man obeyed and grabbed the hair of the body and raised it away from the saddle blanket. For what seemed like an eternity, Sanchez studied the face of Ruiz. He then gestured to the vaquero to lower the head back. He then returned to Fernandez.

'Who did this, Luis? What stinking animal had the nerve to kill our beloved Pedro?'

Fernandez shrugged. 'We do not know, Don Miguel. Pedro was miles ahead of us when we heard two shots. It took hours for us to reach him. He was already dead when we reached him.'

Sanchez gave a heavy sigh.

'What of Pepe and the others?'

'They are following the trail left by the killer. They will hunt him down and make him pay for this violation.'

'Killer? Do you not mean killers, Luis?' Sanchez stared at the body of the man he had thought invincible. 'It would take more than one man to have killed Pedro. It must be the vermin who have infested the valley. The settlers did this.'

Fernandez nodded in agreement. 'You are right, Don Miguel. It must have been the settlers. They must have ambushed Pedro like the cowards they are.'

Sanchez looked at the guards and waved the gun at them. 'Bury him and then prepare our horses. We shall join the hunt for the killers. They will pay with their lives.'

Fernandez made as though to follow the others.

'Where are you going, Luis?' Sanchez enquired.

The vaquero was about to reply when the barrel of the .45 was smashed across his face with brutal force. The sound of cracking teeth filled the courtyard as Fernandez's head was jerked backwards. He fell on to his knees and stared through blurred eyes down at the fragments of teeth on the sand as blood poured from his mouth.

Don Miguel Sanchez smiled.

It was dawn. The brilliant rays of the sun swept across the valley and brought an end to the lingering frost which had only just started to take hold. Mist rose from the valley to the blue heavens above. The two other dirt farmers and their families had gathered together outside Landon's cabin when they had become aware of the stranger who had ridden into their midst. Stan James chewed on a handful of grain as his wife and daughters talked and played with Jose Garcia's large brood. The Mexican sat on the tree stump with a pipe in his mouth and silently stared at the Landon's cabin door.

'Little Billy said that his pa was tending to a real ugly varmint, Jose,' James muttered for the umpteenth time. 'Ugliest critter ever to walk on two legs, the boy reckoned.'

Garcia nodded. 'The boy said that the man looked real mean OK.'

James leaned back and looked up to the chimney and the smoke which still flowed from it. He rubbed his neck and then kicked at the dirt.

'Dan told us not to light our fires 'coz it'll bring them vaqueros down on us,' James grumbled. 'How come he's got his lit, Jose? How come? Damn! I've bin eating cold vittles for a week or more and my guts is plumb hurting. What's Dan thinking about to have smoke rising up like that?'

Garcia nodded. 'I too have a bad belly.'

'Shut the hell up, Jose. Don't ya understand that smoke could bring all of them vaqueros down on us and our families?'

'I understand, Stan.' Garcia sighed. 'I still have a bad belly though.'

Angrily James raised his arm and was about to hammer on the door with his fist. Then he changed his mind and decided to wait a little longer. Dan Landon was too big to make angry.

'When's he coming out to tell us what's going on?'

'I do not know.' Garcia shrugged as some of his children started to chase chickens around the Landon's milk cow. 'I would like to be able to have some nice hot food. I feel so weak.'

Olive James moved to the side of her man. 'Is anything happening, Stan? I'm getting mighty troubled.'

'I don't know, woman,' James snapped.

Garcia rose to his feet and touched the arm of the taller James before pointing to the side of the small cabin.

'Look, Stan. Do you see what I see?'

James turned to where his friend was indicating.
His eyes screwed up when he saw the tall palomino
tied up beneath a canvas sheet spread out from the
building and tied to a couple of saplings.

'Sweet Lord. That's one hell of a horse, Jose.'

Both men moved closer to the powerful creature.
Garcia was first to notice the saddle on the ground.

'Look at this,' he said leaning over and touching
the hand-tooled saddle. 'I think this is the saddle of
a vaquero, not a cowboy.'

'What's that?' James moved closer to the stallion
and saw the brand on the animal's flank. He
touched it and then looked at his pal. 'Ain't that the
same brand we seen on them other vaqueros' nags,
Jose? Ain't that the Sanchez mark?'

Garcia stared and then nodded.

'You are right, amigo. That is one of Don
Miguel's horses.'

James swung on his boots. 'Who in tarnation has
Dan got in there? I sure hope it ain't one of
Sanchez's murderous riders.'

'Me too.'

James looked angry. 'I'm gonna ask Dan about
this.'

Garcia trailed his irate friend back to the door of
the cabin like a hound tracking a bowl of innards.
He watched as James raised his arm and was about
to hit the solid wooden door when it suddenly
opened.

Both men took a step backwards.

Dan Landon was far bigger than either of his neighbours and cast a longer shadow as he stepped out into the morning light. He sighed and then yawned.

'What you two making such a ruckus about? I ain't had me a wink of shuteye all night.'

James tried to look around the side of the well-built man but Landon was far too wide. His eyes looked up into the face of the younger man.

'Who in tarnation ya got in there, Dan? And how come ya got that fire lit? That smoke'll bring them Mex bastards right down on us.'

'How'd you know we have someone in there, Stan?'

'Little Billy told us when he come over to play with my gals, Dan,' James answered.

'Who is it, Dan?' Garcia asked in a whisper.

'A bounty hunter,' Landon replied.

Both men seemed to freeze. They stood like statues as the words drilled their way into their minds.

'A bounty hunter?' James eventually managed to repeat the unexpected words. 'Them hombres are natural born killers, Dan.'

'I too have heard of these men,' Garcia nodded. 'They kill people for money.'

'Outlaws mostly,' Landon added with a smile as he made his way to a water barrel. He scooped two handfuls and splashed it over his face.

Stan James felt himself start to shake. 'You bin tending him, Dan?'

'Yep.' Landon sighed. 'He had a couple of ribs sticking out of his side and I fixed them.'

James looked at Garcia. 'He tended a bloodthirsty killer, Jose. A critter who'll probably kill us all in our sleep.'

Landon walked to the two men and rested his large hands on their shoulders. He leaned down until his head was between theirs and then spoke quietly so that only they could hear his words.

'This man might be our salvation.' he declared.

'Bounty hunters only work for money, Dan.'

'We have no money, amigo.'

Landon looked at the children playing happily. 'I reckon this man will help us. He's already killed one of them vaqueros. That's how he got that palomino.'

Stan James moved to the open doorway and stared into the dark interior. He could not see anything.

'This critter got a handle?'

'He calls himself Iron Eyes,' Landon replied.

James spun on his heels and stared open-mouthed at the big smiling man beside him. He moved to Landon and looked up into the face.

'Iron Eyes?'

Landon nodded. 'Yep. Why? You heard of him?'

James sat down on the tree stump. 'Ain't you heard of him, Dan? I thought everyone knew the name of Iron Eyes.'

'Nope. What's wrong? You look like you just seen a ghost, Stan.'

'I also have heard of this Iron Eyes,' Garcia managed to whisper. 'He has visited my country many times. They say he is the most dangerous of men. Some say that he is already dead.'

Unable to grasp the fear his fellow farmers displayed, Dan Landon rubbed his neck. He was about to speak when he saw the thin emaciated figure in the frame of the cabin doorway. Iron Eyes had a cigar gripped between his teeth. He struck a match and then raised the flame to the black weed. A trail of smoke drifted from his mouth.

'I ain't dead, amigos. I make other folks dead,' Iron Eyes drawled.

TEN

There was a mixed reaction between the two dirt farmers who stared in disbelief at the sight of the tall thin bounty hunter who leaned against the crude doorframe and sucked on the black weed between his gritted teeth. They both had heard tales of the infamous man who stood before them. Tales so tall they could have towered over the mightiest tree within the unnamed valley. Yet the more they stared at the fearsome man, the more they began to realize that all of those stories might actually be true. Dan Landon's neighbours were torn by the revelation that one of the deadliest gunmen in the entire West was within feet of them. One reason for their confusion was that Iron Eyes might just be their saviour, as Landon had whispered. For Iron Eyes had weaponry and knew how to use it to devastating effect.

The second cause for alarm was that this lethal man could also bring about their downfall in one blazing onslaught by the ruthless vaqueros. For both James and Garcia knew that Sanchez could never allow outsiders who entered his own private kingdom to get away with murder. He would be hell-bent on vengeance once he discovered that the bounty hunter had already dispatched one of his vaqueros into the bowels of Hell. None of them would be safe again.

They would all be guilty in the eyes of Sanchez.

Each and every one of the settlers would be punished.

Neither James nor Garcia could actually believe their eyes as they looked at the sight before them. With no shirt to conceal his strapped waist or the battleground of old scars which covered his pitifully lean frame, Iron Eyes barely resembled a human being at all.

This man seemed to have more physical and facial scars than anyone else they had ever encountered. Some of the skin on the bruised and battered frame looked as though it had been melted by fire. They were not to know that that was exactly what Iron Eyes had endured many years earlier.

Above all other things the bounty hunter had proved himself to be a survivor. But even his luck had to run out one day, they quietly assumed.

Iron Eyes inhaled and then stepped out into the morning light. Both James's and Garcia's wives gave a gasp of shocked horror when they saw him.

Yet the children seemed to accept what they saw.

Somehow their young minds had yet to discover the prejudices that most adults grew into. For they did not fear this wounded man and therefore did not brand him as the rest of the country had done. It mattered little to them what colour a person was or how thin or fat some might be. They still had a purity and innocence which did not notice such things.

Yet their mothers rounded them up as mothers do and vainly tried to shield their offspring's eyes from seeing the very thing their own eyes were unable to stop looking at. Without even knowing it, they were fuelling their children's souls with the seeds of their own fear.

Seeds which would take root and grow.

But one of the children refused to be pulled into the calico skirts of his mother. Little Billy was like his father and just watched the tall figure with interest and curiosity.

Iron Eyes reached the barrel and scooped up some of the water in his left hand and rubbed it over his face. He shook like a dog emerging from a river and the wet strands of limp hair dangled down over his brutalized face. He stared at the people who surrounded him.

They were a helpless bunch, he thought.

Incapable of protecting themselves.

Even wounded, Iron Eyes knew that he was far more capable of surviving in this wild land than any of the onlookers. Perhaps it was because he had no female in tow. Maybe it was because he had no children of his own to protect.

Death held no fear for someone who had ridden with it on his shoulder for an entire lifetime.

Silently the bounty hunter knew that he would probably outlast all of them. For they had a weakness. They required one another whilst he required nobody except himself. He had long wondered why men of all colours desired to be chained down by the burden of families.

It made no sense to him.

He dropped the cigar and pushed his mule-eared boot down upon it until the smoke was crushed into the mud. His eyes still looked at those who kept watching his every movement.

Stan James cleared his throat, found a little courage from somewhere and pointed up at the smoking chimney.

'Why'd you light that fire, Dan?'

'Iron Eyes needed some hot vittles.'

'But look at that smoke.'

Landon glanced upward briefly. 'Yeah, it is smoking a tad too much, Stan.'

Iron Eyes did not speak. He picked up a wooden pail from the ground and scooped a gallon of water from the barrel. He then walked slowly back towards the door. Just as he was about to enter the cabin again he paused and tilted his head.

His eyes burned at James.

'What was that ya said about the smoke, friend?'

James felt his face twitch. His eyes darted around the others before finding those of the bounty hunter, who waited for a reply like a vulture waiting for something to die.

'I . . . I said that the chimney is making a lotta smoke.'

'Don't ya like smoke?' Iron Eyes asked.

James shrugged nervously. 'I . . . I just thought that the smoke might bring them vaqueros down on us. That's all.'

Iron Eyes nodded. 'Reckon ya right. Smoke might bring the whole bunch of them down on us like a pack of hungry wolves. In fact I'm certain it will do just that.'

Stan James smiled. He thought that his reasoning had seemed correct to the stranger who had come to visit their small community.

James had been quite right.

Every eye watched Iron Eyes as he moved into the cabin towards the smouldering embers of the fire. Then to their utter amazement they watched the bounty hunter raise and then pour the pail of water over the fire.

Instantly the cabin was filled with choking smoke. Even more of the black smoke rose up through the chimney and billowed up into the sky. It was a hundred times more dense than previously.

'What you do?' Garcia asked.

'He's loco!' James yelled out in horror.

'Now even a blind man will be able to find this place,' Garcia added.

'We're done for.'

Iron Eyes tossed the pail out towards the watching men, then reached down to the cot and picked up his guns. He stuffed them into his pants belt and picked up his bloodstained coat. He slid it on and then followed the pail.

He grinned the twisted grin that only his face could manage. He rested a hand on the doorframe again and shook his head as smoke curled all around him.

Landon rushed up to Iron Eyes.

'Why'd you do that? They'll know exactly where we are and come to kill us.'

Iron Eyes stared into the eyes of the big man. 'That's what I want 'em to do, Dan. I want them to come here coz I'm too tuckered to go looking for them.'

'What?' Landon gasped.

'When ya hunting two-legged critters ya gotta bait the things. Make the bastards think they're on top. Draw them into ya trap and then finish the job.' Iron Eyes said coldly.

'You want them to find our cabins?' Landon asked.

'Yep.'

Landon rubbed his neck with his powerful hands. 'They'll kill us all, Iron Eyes.'

'Maybe.'

'You don't understand. Don Miguel Sanchez has maybe fifty men, Iron Eyes,' Landon told him. 'Can you kill that many?'

Iron Eyes took a deep breath and then saw the blue eyes of the courageous boy looking straight at him.

'I've killed more.' he admitted.

ELEVEN

The blistering sun had barely cleared the steep rocks which flanked both sides of the valley but even its fiery heat was nothing compared to that which burned inside the heartless soul of the ruthless Sanchez. The drawbridge lowered from the whitewashed hacienda and a few seconds later Don Miguel Sanchez, astride his white stallion, thundered through its arched portal ahead of the thirty-two well-armed vaqueros. It was the first time for more than five years that he had ridden with his men but that was because there had never been any real threat to his empire before.

They raced down from the hacienda with the military precision of a swarm of soldier ants. Like the deadly insects they too would try to find and overwhelm their enemy. The magnificent horses carried their masters into the depths of the valley.

Riding in all his finery the Spaniard looked every inch the nobleman he claimed to be as he led his small army along the well-trodden trail beside the fast-flowing water. He had left a mere eight vaqueros and guards in the hacienda to protect his stronghold.

Sanchez wanted to impose his authority.

This had little to do with vengeance for Pedro Ruiz and more to do with proving his power not only to the people who dared challenge his right to this beautiful land but to his own band of heavily armed followers.

Fear kept men like Sanchez in power. It was something he had learned long ago back in his homeland.

Countless cattle scattered and ran into the high grass as the horsemen galloped north through their pastures. Sanchez narrowed his eyes and steered his mount into the creek, then spurred hard. Water flew up over the stallion and cooled them both. It had been a long time since he had ventured along the entire length of the valley and he knew that it would take the better part of a day to cover the ground even on his own specially bred horses.

Someone had killed Ruiz but the vainglorious horseman gave the killer little thought. To him this was just a grand show of his might. In his mind they would find the culprits easily and execute them without mercy. He was not leading the majority of his men towards battle; this was going to be a massacre.

Don Miguel Sanchez glanced over his shoulder at

the men who rode behind him. He then returned his gaze to the trail ahead. With a whip in his left hand he lashed the powerful shoulders of the white stallion. The horse found more pace.

Sanchez smiled.

The stallion charged on through the creek. The vaqueros mounts followed at matching speed. Every one of them imagined that this was going to be little more than a well-polished turkey shoot.

None of them knew towards what or whom they were blindly racing. If they had they might have slowed their pace.

There was a war awaiting them at the end of the valley.

A two-legged war.

Its name was Iron Eyes.

Iron Eyes had faced down entire gangs before with little more than two guns and dogged courage to protect him. Yet this was a whole lot different, he thought. For the first time he had the lives of innocent people in his hands. These were not people who knew how to fight anything harsher than the elements and the ever-changing seasons. Yet there were those who wanted them dead and they had no way of protecting themselves. None of them had any weaponry and of them all there were just three grown men.

Landon had mentioned that the mysterious Sanchez had fifty vaqueros on his payroll. Iron Eyes knew that time was running out fast for these hard-working people.

If muscles could defeat bullets, Iron Eyes would have had faith in Landon, James and Garcia. But muscles could not prevent death when it spewed from the barrels of guns and there were guns aplenty headed their way.

That was something Iron Eyes knew for certain. Although the big Dan Landon had said that the farmers' troubles had started long before he had even entered the valley, Iron Eyes felt that he was responsible, because of his killing of the vaquero. Guilt was an emotion new to the bounty hunter.

It did not sit well with him.

Every eye watched him as he walked around the cabin and surveyed the area which surrounded them. Every step brought even more doubts to those who watched. But Iron Eyes was not so easily deterred from his belief in his own ability to defeat anyone foolhardy enough to go up against him.

He paused beside the three females and their brood of children. His eyes looked at the dirty faces of the boys and girls before darting to the trio of troubled farmers.

He drew a cigar from his pocket, pushed it between his teeth and chewed on it as he paced up to Landon and the other two. For minutes he did not speak as the black weed moved between his cracked and scarred lips.

The three men could not hide their concern

from the bounty hunter. The smoke still curled into the blue sky from the chimney like an Indian smoke signal but Iron Eyes was not worried by their lack of faith in him. He had enough for them all. Without uttering a word Iron Eyes lowered his skeletal hands into both of the trail-coat's deep pockets. His bony fingers separated the cigars from the bullets until he was able to scoop every single one of his .36 calibre shells out into the morning light. His eyes narrowed as he stared at the bullets.

'What's wrong?' Landon queried.

'Ain't enough,' Iron Eyes eventually mumbled.

Landon stepped closer. 'Don't you have any more ammunition, Iron Eyes?'

Iron Eye's gaze bored into the farmer's eyes.

'Nope,' he answered. 'I figured that I wouldn't need any more than this to kill the outlaw I've bin chasing. Never figured on this trouble.'

Landon held on to the hands of the man before him as he roughly counted the bullets they held. He then looked up and said the number aloud.

'Twenty-one.'

Iron Eyes nodded, dropped the bullets back into the deep pockets and then touched the grips of his Navy Colts.

'I got me twelve more in my guns,' he calculated. 'I figure that makes thirty-three. Ain't nearly enough if that Sanchez critter has as many vaqueros as you say he has.'

'Then we're doomed,' James blurted out. 'Doomed.'

'I knew making the smoke was a mistake.' Garcia almost cried.

Landon leaned close to Iron Eyes. 'What'll we do? If you ain't got enough bullets to fend them varmints off, we're finished, like Stan reckons.'

Iron Eyes produced a match from somewhere and scratched its tip with a thumbnail. He inhaled the smoke of the cigar deeply and gave the area another hard look. If the bounty hunter was worried, it sure did not show.

'First thing ya gotta do is get these women and young'uns away from here,' he said.

Landon turned and raised a hand to point.

'There are caves at the foot of the rocks.' he said. 'We stored a lot of things there when we first come to this valley. Stuff we wanted to protect in case them vaqueros found our cabins.'

Iron Eyes tilted his head back. 'What kinda stuff?'

'Wagons and things,' Landon added. 'We figured it would be safer to keep the big stuff in or close to the caves.'

'Anything else? Maybe dynamite or something?'

Landon shook his head and then paused as his memory recalled something he had forgotten. His eyes focused on the emotionless figure who sucked on the cigar.

'Hold on a minute. One of the dirt farmers who come in with us was named Seth Hogan. Him and his family was killed by the vaqueros. He had black powder in a few barrels that he'd figured he could use for blowing up tree-stumps. Trouble is it was always too dangerous to use the powder in case it brought those vaqueros down on us. Seth never got to use any of that powder. It must be still up at the caves.'

'Black powder, huh?' Iron Eyes was thoughtful.

James stepped towards the two men. 'It still has to be there on the flatbed of his old wagon, Dan. There was five small barrels of the stuff as I recall.'

'That's right. Five barrels,' Landon agreed.

Iron Eyes scratched his cheek. 'I ain't never used black powder before but its gotta be easier and safer than sticks of dynamite. That stuff can be darn tricky if ya get the length of the fuse wire wrong.'

Landon looked at their familes and then back at the man with the smouldering weed between his teeth.

'When do you figure we should head on up to the caves, Iron Eyes?'

'I figure about now would be a damn smart time to start,' the bounty hunter snapped back at the large man. 'I got me a feeling that trouble is coming in fast now I've sent up that smoke signal.'

'You heard him, Dan. Let's go,' James urged.

Iron Eyes sucked on the cigar and stared through its grey smoke. He nodded at James.

Landon moved to the other men. 'You heard him. Git the women and kids out of here, boys. Take the milk cows and enough provisions to last a couple of days.'

With great relief James and Garcia did exactly as Landon had instructed. As they saw it they had been given the one thing they both wanted and that was to flee.

The bounty hunter stared curiously at Landon, who was watching the others.

'Ain't ya going as well, Dan?' Iron Eyes asked.

'Nope. I'm gonna help you fight off them vaqueros,' Landon said.

Iron Eyes shook his head slowly in obvious disagreement. 'No you ain't. Ya ain't even got a gun and this is gonna be a blood-bath to end all blood-baths. Git going. I ain't got time to teach ya how to duck bullets.'

'But I ain't scared.'

'It ain't a matter of being scared or not, Dan,' the bounty hunter explained. 'I need you to herd them others up to them caves. I'll come looking for ya when I'm through here.'

'You figuring on using the black powder?'

Iron Eyes inhaled on the cigar again. 'It'll be our last line of defence as them soldier boys up north say. If Don Miguel Sanchez is the kinda locobean I reckon he is, we'll need that powder to finish this once and for all.'

Reluctantly Dan Landon left the side of the thin man and joined the others on their exodus.

Iron Eyes pulled one of his guns from his belt

and cocked its hammer. He knew that there were riders headed to this secret place hidden within the woods. The smoke was a bait they could not resist. Every ounce of his honed hunting instincts told him his prey was getting closer.

'Reckon I better try and get me a few more guns,' he muttered to himself as he silently made his way into the dense brush.

Turning away from his wife and child, Dan Landon went to ask Iron Eyes something. To his utter surprise the man was gone.

TWELVE

Joe Brewster knew that something was wrong in this apparent paradise. Very wrong. He had found refuge in the beautiful valley in an attempt to escape the relentless bounty hunter who, he knew, would die rather than give up his intention to add him to his tally of dead wanted outlaws. Yet the place Brewster had thought would be a peaceful and safe place to hide was anything but. Just like the vaqueros and farmers, he too had heard the gunfire the previous day and wondered who had squeezed those triggers. Unlike the others though, the outlaw had no desire to go and find out. He knew that it might have been another of the tricks the bounty hunter employed to lure the naïve into his web of death.

The creek which ran along the length of the valley would have been an easy way to travel from its northern end to the distant south but Brewster knew that that would have given Iron Eyes an easy target. Joe Brewster had already seen what the infamous hunter of men had done to his brothers and did not want to join them in the bowels of Hell too soon.

The outlaw had seen Iron Eyes fall wounded when he had fired a volley of deadly lead at him back at Rio Valdo. Anyone else would have quit his pursuit, but not the hideous bounty hunter. He had somehow managed to keep on coming after him.

Brewster remembered his utter shock when he had glanced behind him and seen the rider still following him.

The outlaw knew that if he were to have any chance of escaping the certain death of finding himself in Iron Eyes's gun sights he had to stay in the woods and eventually try to navigate a way down into the Mexican heartland.

A thousand trees and the dense undergrowth would have to be his shield, his only protection from Iron Eyes's lethal accuracy. Yet Brewster had already learned that this was no easy place through which to ride. After hiding in the dense woodland for nearly a whole day he had finally decided to try his luck and start out on his bid for freedom.

He had to escape. Time was running out and every nerve and sinew of his body told him so.

But this place was far more dangerous than he had imagined when his eyes first saw the unexpected valley from the high desert ridge.

All day he had seen and heard riders as they

travelled through the fast-moving waters of the wide creek. Something was definitely wrong and he did not want to get involved in anything which might hamper his attempt to escape Iron Eyes's vengefulness. Brewster had not recognized any of the horsemen but knew what hired gunmen looked like, whatever their nationality. The vaqueros were heavily armed and obviously looking for someone or something to kill.

He knew that it could not be his hide they sought as only one man knew that he had entered the valley, but that did not make him sit any easier on his rested mount. They were gunning for someone and after escaping Iron Eyes he prayed that he would not get caught in the middle of other men's lethal crossfire. The ruthless Brewster knew how to kill but he was no fighter. His breed were back-shooters. Nothing more and nothing less.

So far his luck had saved him. Yet luck can be bad as well as good, he told himself.

Brewster steadied the horse beneath him and patted the saddle-bags. They were swollen with the money he and his dead brothers had stolen down in San Remus. Now it was all his and he wanted to spend every damn penny of it.

He tapped his spurs and moved away from the small clearing where he had spent so many hours chewing on jerky and hardtack and began his journey once more.

As the horse began the difficult walk between the

trees his mind raced. A thought came to the outlaw. One which made him smile.

Maybe those Mexican gunfighters were after Iron Eyes. It was a thought which gave him the courage to continue onward.

Pepe Gomez was no tracker but even he could not fail to see the unmistakable hoof tracks left by the palomino stallion ridden by the unknown man who had bettered Pedro Ruiz. The tracks had led away from where they had discovered Ruiz's body, across the muddy bank of the creek and into the wood. The vaquero had led his six companions across the almost trackless ground. Only one animal had travelled this route in days and that was the palomino.

The sun filtered through the tree canopies and was on their backs but none of them seemed to notice. Each of them knew that somewhere ahead death awaited them. They continued trailing the elusive horseman with only one thought between them.

They knew that they would not only have to find their prey but they would have to kill him as well. Don Miguel Sanchez would expect nothing less than a trophy to calm his anger. A head to place on a pike upon the high walls of his hacienda. A carcass to skin and nail to the drawbridge as a warning to all others who dared to enter the forbidden Eden.

When the seven horsemen had set out just after

dawn it had seemed an easy task to achieve. Seven men to kill just one. The longer they had ridden the more their mutual doubts had grown.

They had begun to realize that this was no ordinary man they were hunting.

Who was it who could get the better of Ruiz with a single shot? Whoever it was, the man was brave. No coward had fired that lethal shot.

The bushes and trees were getting harder and harder for the seven horsemen to negotiate. Everything green seemed to be entangled in thorn-covered brambles. Barbed wire created by nature itself. Progress had become slow and painful. The further they travelled the more difficult it was for their sturdy mounts to find ways through the unyielding undergrowth. These were prized horses and none of the vaqueros wanted them to be scarred or ripped apart by the savagely thorny vegetation.

Iron Eyes, on the other hand, had spurred and driven onwards the powerful stallion beneath him without a second thought for the animal's welfare.

Every drop of sweat reminded Gomez that they had to continue their search for, even though they were all weary of the chase, their fear of returning to Sanchez without the killer was even more terrifying. Gomez knew that it would be their heads on pikes should they fail in their mission. Nothing less would appease Sanchez.

Gomez rode at the head of the seven riders. As they emerged from the woods it was he who kept his eyes upon the soft fertile soil. He who followed the tracks left by the stallion's hoofs.

The seven vaqueros rode up a small rise and then saw the one thing that they had spent days searching for. All the horsemen reined in and stared in disbelief across the tops of the trees at the black smoke which could still be seen twisting up into the blue sky miles ahead of them.

Gomez lifted a hand and pointed.

'Look. Smoke,' he declared.

The other vaqueros remained silent as they too stared at the smoke. Each man wondered who it was who had suddenly allowed smoke to rise into the heavens.

Was it the last of the settlers?

Or was it the unknown gunman whose trail they had followed for so long?

Gomez turned and looked at another of the men called Antonio Picario. Picario was almost thirty and, unlike his fellow vaqueros, wore two guns. He could use them both with equal accuracy.

'What do you think, Antonio?' Gomez asked.

'I think it is smoke,' came the insolent reply.

'But who has made this smoke?'

'Whoever it is I think we should kill him.'

Gomez nodded in agreement.

Suddenly, to their total surprise, a hundred yards ahead of them the vaqueros saw a fleeting glimpse of someone moving behind a line of trees.

'There he is,' one of the horsemen announced,

dragging his pistol from its holster.

Gomez held on to his reins tightly. He had seen the figure but it was a long way from where the smoke was rising.

'It does not make any sense, amigos. How could the smoke be over there and the rider down in the trees?'

There was no time for reply.

Suddenly a Winchester opened up from between two of the trees. The sound of the shots came a split second after bullets tore into them. Horses reared up as two riders were blasted from their saddles. More shots followed. The horses whinnied in alarm. Gomez spun his mount as another volley of bullets cut into them again.

His eyes were wide open and unblinking. A pain unlike anything he had ever felt before cut into him.

Gomez hit the ground hard.

Seeing Gomez on the ground, Picario drew both his guns and cocked their hammers. Gomez managed to force himself up on one elbow.

'Take cover, Antonio,' Gomez coughed.

But mere words of caution were not what hot-blooded men like Picario wanted to hear. His was a far simpler solution. In his view only cowards would take cover.

'Come on, my brothers. Let us make this dog pay,' the vaquero screamed at the others. He started to fire back at the man who still cocked and fired his rifle at them. The vaqueros spurred and drove on down the hill. Their murderous chants filled the woods.

Steering the animal with the power of his legs alone Picario cocked and fired each gun in turn as his three fellow riders spread out.

A haze of gunsmoke spread across the clearing, filling the gunmen's nostrils with its acrid stench. No longer could they see the target of the vengeance they wished to dish out.

All four riders were within twenty yards of the rifleman when Picario too felt the powerful impact of the bullets which cut through him. The young vaquero was lifted off his saddle like a rag doll. He rolled over the cantle of his saddle and fell. He seemed to float in the air for an eternity as his mount raced on without him. When he hit the lush grass it was obvious he was dead.

The others continued shooting and charging down to where the plumes of rifle smoke still hung on the warm air.

The three horsemen hauled rein and blasted their guns at the gap between the two trees.

There was no reply.

No return of fire.

The rifleman was no longer there.

As their hammers fell on spent casings and their gunsmoke slowly cleared the vaqueros realized that their attacker had gone.

Joe Brewster was already a hundred yards away.

He was spurring his mount away from the clearing and what was left of the vaqueros.

Unknown to the vicious outlaw, his route would take him directly to a more deadly place.

And a far more deadly enemy.

THIRTEEN

With both Navy Colts gripped firmly in his bony hands, Iron Eyes stood motionless like a granite statue. Nothing on the skeletal figure moved except his mane of long hair. He tried to work out which direction the sound of gunfire he had heard moments earlier might have come from. Then the bounty hunter knew the answer. Flocks of birds had risen up into the heavens directly north of where he stood. He tilted his head back and watched them fly overhead. Iron Eyes's keen hunting instincts told him that birds always flew away from gunfire.

The thicket was dense and trees surrounded him on all sides, but that did not matter to the bounty hunter. All his concentration was upon the sounds of the brief battle which continued to ring in his ears. He lowered his guns and then slid them both into his belt beneath the fresh bandages made from Wilma Landon's petticoats.

The cold steel chilled his belly. It sharpened his

115

thoughts like a wetstone on a knife's edge.

His expert knowledge of all types of weaponry had already informed him that one rifle had taken on at least half a dozen six-shooters. He had already seen one vaquero's arsenal and knew that for some reason the Mexicans, like himself, seemed to favour handguns over rifles.

The question which burned into his mind like a branding-iron was a simple one.

Who had fired the rifle?

Then he recalled Joe Brewster, the outlaw for whom he was determined to claim the bounty money. He had a rifle. Even wounded, Iron Eyes had seen it in its saddle scabbard when the outlaw had high-tailed it out of Rio Valdo.

Iron Eyes rubbed his chin.

Could it have been other vaqueros who had fought with Brewster? According to the burly Dan Landon the valley was crawling with them. The longer he dwelled upon the theory the more it made sense. Who else would they be fighting? Iron Eyes knew that by now they must have discovered the dead body he had left upon the muddy banks of the creek. If they had bumped into the outlaw they would naturally think that he had killed the vaquero. It certainly could not be any of the farmers who were shooting. The farmers were unarmed and far off in the opposite direction.

'Brewster.' Iron Eyes allowed the name to escape his lips.

116

The gaunt man had only briefly encountered Joe Brewster but he knew that the outlaw liked to bushwhack folks. He was not the sort to take anyone on face to face. Outlaws were basically cowards and never got involved in showdowns.

Iron Eyes lowered his head thoughtfully. A smile crossed the scarred face.

With everything that had happened to him since he had gunned down the vaquero, Iron Eyes had almost forgotten the reason he was here in the first place.

He was here to kill the last of the Brewster clan.

No other reason. Dead or alive meant only dead to Iron Eyes.

The twisted smile grew wider. Then thoughts of losing the reward money filled his mind and ended the smile. What if they had killed the outlaw?

His reward money could be lying dead out there someplace, he thought. His teeth gritted.

An urgency overwhelmed him. He had to discover the truth.

He glanced keenly all around him. Iron Eyes took a step forward. The brush was unyielding but nature had never been able to stop his progress before. He bent down and plucked the long Bowie knife from the neck of his right boot. His cold eyes stared at the knife. The dried blood of so many outlaws and Indians filled its scratched back above the Nazer sharp-edged blade.

He gripped its handle and then swung it like a

sabre and saw the tangle of thorny brambles fall away.

The bounty hunter hacked with sweeping strokes until he had managed to cover an extra hundred or so yards into the depths of the woods.

He then paused once more and listened.

He could hear a horse labouring through the distant maze of trees and vicious brush. With every beat of the bounty hunter's cold heart the sound of the animal grew louder in his hunter's ears. It was a long way away but Iron Eyes could hear it approaching.

He closed his eyes and concentrated.

Knowingly, Iron Eyes nodded to himself. The rider was using the woodland and not the far easier creek to travel down the valley. That meant only one thing.

It was the outlaw.

Joe Brewster was still alive.

There was still a fighting chance of claiming the bounty on the outlaw's head. Iron Eyes relaxed.

His thoughts returned to the plight of the farmers he had vowed to help. The bounty hunter slid the knife back into his boot, turned and retraced his steps between the trees. He was heading for Dan Landon's small cabin. From there he would trail the dirt farmers and their families up to the distant rockface.

There was black powder to obtain.

There was a trap to set.

A trap for far bigger prey than the last of the Brewster brothers. It took almost an hour but he knew that the outlaw would not be able to move as fast as he could. The trees were too close together for the most part. His lean frame could slip between them easily. Brewster's horse could not. Iron Eyes had discovered that when he had ridden through the woods astride the palomino stallion.

It was late afternoon when Iron Eyes reached the cabin. He then moved silently to the palomino stallion. He threw a blanket on its back and then the hefty Mexican saddle. He reached under the horse's belly and grabbed the cinch straps. He buckled the straps, then lifted his saddle-bags up and tossed them behind the cantle. He used the cantle's leather laces and secured the bags.

Iron Eyes held on to the saddle horn, poked his left boot toe into the stirrup and hauled his lean frame up until he was able to throw his right leg over the broad back of the nervous animal. He tore the reins free and then gathered them up in his hands.

It would not take long to reach Landon and the others, he told himself. They were on foot and herding milk cows and children up to the base of the steep rock walls. The stallion would make short time of the journey that they had to toil to complete.

Iron Eyes turned the stallion and spurred.

The golden animal thundered up into the woods.

It sounded like a hundred heavenly thunderclaps exploding one after another along the valley. Yet no mere thunderstorm could have created a more fearsome noise than did the hoofs of the vaqueros' magnificent horses as they continued on their vengeful quest.

The sun had fallen behind the towering rocks but night would not arrive for another two hours yet. Until then an eerie half-light would fill the valley as the sky slowly turned crimson above the horsemen. They had driven their mounts hard and without rest for most of the day but now even the powerful white stallion beneath Sanchez was beginning to flag.

Reluctantly Don Miguel Sanchez brought his thirty or so followers to a halt. The exhausted vaqueros dismounted beside their equally worn-out mounts.

Only Sanchez remained defiantly atop his horse.

Like an eagle searching for its prey his eyes narrowed and stared out into the fading light of the lush valley. The creek was wide and the trees to either side of its fast-moving waters appeared almost impenetrable. The Spaniard eased himself off the stallion and remained at the horse's noble head as others rushed around the scene. His entire body hurt but he would never allow his men to see the pain which racked his body. For men of aristocratic breeding had a duty to their underlings to maintain the illusion of their superiority.

His features remained the same as he continued to search for those who had infiltrated his empire. No emotion apart from anger ever changed his chiselled, Latin looks. The horses were spent but the ride was far from over, Sanchez told himself. It could not end until he had the bodies of those who had dared to challenge his authority.

Exactly like the ancient rulers of the Old World from which he had come, Sanchez ruled by might and fear. There was no mercy in the blood which flowed through his veins.

Sanchez raised a hand and snapped his fingers. Men came rushing to his side.

'Break out the grain, amigos. We shall allow the horses to eat and rest,' Sanchez informed them coldly. 'Make a fire and cook some food.'

The vaqueros began to carry out their instructions.

Sanchez defied his aching bones and screaming muscles and walked a few yards ahead of his men and their mounts. He kept looking down the valley. There were less than ten miles left before the valley gave way to the desert. Somewhere along this strip of land between the high rockfaces to either side of the valley there were people he knew he had to destroy.

But where?

Where were they?

Sanchez looked back at his men. 'Before the stars fill the sky we shall be back in our saddles.'

FOURTEEN

The palomino stallion moved as though it had nobody in its saddle on its approach to the rockface. The bounty hunter was so light that apart from the spurs which repeatedly jabbed into its flanks the animal might have thought it had thrown the rider. The trail had been easy for Iron Eyes to follow. That single fact troubled the thin emaciated horseman. For if he could trail these people so easily then others might be able to do exactly the same. He drew back on his reins and stopped the powerful stallion just ahead of the sturdy Dan Landon. Landon stood like a tree before his people. Iron Eyes looked at the high rockface before him. It stretched out in both directions as far as the eye could see.

To his surprise the caves were far bigger than he had imagined. Big enough to hold entire wagons.

Iron Eyes carefully looped his long right leg over the neck of his horse and then slid from his saddle to the ground. Even the slight impact of the ground beneath his boots caused pain to rip through the thin body of the bounty hunter.

He paused for a few seconds until it passed and then looked down at the bandages which were strapped around his pitiful torso holding his broken ribs in check. To his utter relief there was no fresh blood on the white fabric.

Iron Eyes looked across at the faces of the men, women and children. Every one of them seemed to be looking back at the bounty hunter as though he might just be able to solve all their troubles with the stroke of a magic wand. But Iron Eyes had no magic wand and was beginning to wonder if his dogged grit might not be enough.

'You OK, Iron Eyes?' Landon asked.

Iron Eyes nodded. 'So far.'

The children were still playing their innocent games around the area. They were blissfully unaware of the dangers which lurked all around them. Dangers which were getting closer with each passing moment.

It worried the tall thin man. Iron Eyes had seen many dead people in his time but he had never become used to the sight of dead children. He silently vowed that he would try his utmost to prevent these children being slaughtered.

Iron Eyes handed his reins to Billy Landon, then followed the child's burly father towards the towering cliff face. A few abandoned wagons were

124

there just inside the nearest of the cave mouths. Then he saw the small barrels of black powder nestled on the flatbed of the closest wagon.

'Five barrels just like you said.' Iron Eyes rested a hand on the tailgate.

'That enough?' Landon asked.

'If it ain't we're all headed to Hell, pard,' Iron Eyes replied. He nodded. He looked around the small clearing at the foot of the steep wall of rock. He studied the scene carefully. It was so peaceful and yet he knew that soon that peace would be shattered by those who sought not only the farmers and their kinfolk but the man who had bettered the vaquero. His mind raced as he thought of the explosive black powder and what he could do with it. So many deadly choices.

'What should we do now, Iron Eyes?' Landon asked.

The bounty hunter looked straight at Landon. 'Is there any way that I might be able to get up this hunk of rock, Dan?'

Landon tilted his head. 'What you wanna do that for?'

Iron Eyes looked upward. 'I wanna get me a better look at this valley,' he answered. 'I figure that the higher I can get the more I'll see.'

Landon edged closer. 'You reckon that the vaqueros are headed this way?'

Iron Eyes nodded slowly. 'Yep. Trouble is I can't be certain unless I get up high so I can see this whole valley. I reckon Sanchez will have to head along the creek to make good time and if so I ought to be able to see him and his guns from up there.'

Dan Landon rubbed the sweat from his face on the back of his muscular right arm and screwed up his eyes.

'You ain't in no fit state to go mountain climbing, Iron Eyes.'

The bounty hunter smiled. 'I know that but there ain't no other way for me to be sure of things. Tell me, can I git up there or not? Is there an easy way to climb this rock?'

Landon looked at his feet. 'I reckon there is but it'll hurt you bad.'

'Hell, I already am hurting bad, Dan,' Iron Eyes admitted.

'C'mon.' Landon shrugged and started to walk away from the others. 'There is an easy way up these rocks down yonder. I'll show you.'

The two men walked for more than twenty minutes along the foot of the sheer cliff face until Landon stopped and raised a finger. He pointed.

Iron Eyes paused and looked at the boulders bathed in the last of the sun's rays. They were weathered stones but looked like a giant staircase which led up the side of the wall of rocks. The thin fingers ran through the long damp hair as Iron Eyes deliberated.

'Will I be able to get to the top?'

'Halfway maybe.'

'Good enough.'

The bounty hunter started the climb. Landon followed.

FIFTEEN

A stiff breeze swept across the face of the high rocks. It blew the long matted hair off the hideous face of the bounty hunter. Iron Eyes stopped and balanced against the wall of rock as Landon reached his side. They were barely fifty feet up but it was enough to give both men uninterrupted views of the entire length of the valley. The treetops looked like one solid entity from that high vantage point. Iron Eyes remained silent as if waiting for his prey to walk into sight. His eyes sharpened against the fading light.

A lifetime had created him until he was the most dangerous of creatures. A hunter.

Landon was about to speak but was stopped by the bony hand which covered his mouth. The dirt farmer screwed up his eyes and stared hard at the man beside him on the narrow ledge. He had never known anyone like Iron Eyes before. He did not speak. He just watched Iron Eyes.

Even though the sky had become black and a myriad stars now sparkled high above them, the hunter of men continued to search the entire valley with eyes which were keener than those of any ordinary man.

Was it possible for anyone to see anything out there in the darkness which had overwhelmed the valley, Landon silently wondered. Landon himself could hardly make out where the tops of the trees ended and the creek began.

'There,' Iron Eyes said flatly.

'You seen something?' Landon asked.

Slowly Iron Eyes raised his left arm and pointed a long thin finger to their right. Landon edged closer to the bounty hunter and stared directly along the pointing finger until he was gazing out beyond the canopy of treetops.

'See 'em?' Iron Eyes asked in a low cold drawl.

For a moment the farmer did not answer. His eyes were attempting to focus. Then he saw light briefly dance across the surface of the distant water.

'What is that, Iron Eyes?'

'A camp-fire,' came the swift reply.

'I don't see a fire.'

'Me neither.' Iron Eyes lowered his arm. 'But I can see what the fire lights up, Dan.'

Landon returned his attention to the man next to him. 'What you trying to tell me?'

'Them vaqueros have lit themselves a fire to cook grub, Dan,' the bounty hunter told him. 'I can't see the fire either, coz the trees are in the way but I can see the light from it dancing on that creek and the men who are moving around it. Look hard.'

'How'd you know they're cooking?'

Iron Eyes sniffed at the air. 'Smell that? That's real good Mexican vittles. That ain't no bacon or hardtack they're rustling up, Dan.'

'Don Miguel Sanchez's men?'

'Reckon so.' Iron Eyes pointed back along the narrow line of boulders they had used to reach this high place. 'Start moving downhill. I've seen all I need to see.'

They both moved slowly down the steep trail towards the ground. It was like finding stepping-stones in a stream. They had to stretch their legs in order to reach each one in turn. It was a difficult descent, made no easier by the darkness.

Landon jumped down the last six feet. He turned and watched the bounty hunter move far more carefully. Iron Eyes reached the ground and then paused for a few seconds.

'What's wrong?' Landon queried.

'I want ya to hitch my horse between the traces of one of them wagons, Dan,' Iron Eyes said. 'The one with them kegs of black powder on the flat bed.'

Landon rubbed his neck. 'That's a mighty heavy wagon there, Iron Eyes. It might cripple that horse of yours.'

'So? I can always git another horse.'

Landon watched the eerie, thin man start back

for the caves and the rest of the people who had gathered there. He could not understand this man.

The bounty hunter walked slowly as though every step hurt.

'You gonna blow them critters up?' Landon eventually managed to ask.

Iron Eyes looked over his wide shoulder. The starlight caught his legendary eyes.

'Like I told ya before, I'll use the powder as a last resort.'

'What comes first on your agenda then?'

'Hell. I'm gonna set fire to ya houses first,' Iron Eyes replied. 'That'll bring them all to me.'

'Burn our homes?' Landon gasped.

Iron Eyes carried on walking.

SIXTEEN

Iron Eyes had only just finished unharnessing his stallion from between the wagon's traces outside the small cabin when he heard a noise to his left. A noise he recognized. Every sinew in his thin body told him someone was coming. The darkness enabled him to move unseen to the palomino's neck. His eyes narrowed as they searched for whoever had made the sound that had alerted his keen senses.

Then he saw them. The trees and brush were dense but enough starlight managed to penetrate the tops of the trees for him to spot the three outlines. A trio of riders astride horses was getting closer by the second.

Silently he drew one of his Navy Colts from his belt and in one fluid motion cocked its hammer.

Iron Eyes moved like a phantom away from the tired horse towards the line of trees, silently and with purpose. Every step brought him closer to the approaching horsemen. They were upwind and he could smell their stale sweat in his flared nostrils.

He paused. His eyes screwed up until they were almost closed as he stared unblinking at the three shapes. Even the dim starlight could not hide their distinctive headwear from his keen vision.

Sombreros.

They were vaqueros.

For a moment Iron Eyes wondered why they were coming from the north and not the south like the others he had spotted from the cliff wall earlier. Then his curiosity waned. It did not matter which direction they were coming from, he told himself. They were vaqueros like the one who had tried and failed to kill him. That single fact had signed their death warrent.

Ignoring the sharp thorns of the tangled briers wrapped around the trunks of tall trees Iron Eyes pushed his thin frame forward and raised his cocked weapon. He felt the thorns rip at his flesh and blood start to trace down his lean body but it did not stop him.

Suddenly the weary horsemen saw him. A horrific figure bathed in the sort of eerie light only found in woods at night.

Startled, they dragged their guns from their holsters but it was already far too late. Faster than any other gunslinger could have acted the bounty hunter fanned his deadly Navy Colt's hammer three times. He stood firm as their horses reared up and shook their lifeless burdens from their backs before scattering into the woods.

Iron Eyes pushed the smoking barrel of his gun back into his belt and walked to each of the dead vaqueros. He plucked their guns from their hands and dropped each of them in turn into his deep trail-coat pockets.

The emotionless Iron Eyes was about to return to his horse and the wagon in the small clearing when he spotted one of the dead vaqueros' mounts a mere twenty feet from where he stood. His eyes narrowed and focused through the bluish half-light which filtered down over the scene at the bags tied behind the high saddle cantle.

A thought came to him.

More quickly than blinking he pulled one of his guns back out from his belt, cocked its hammer, aimed and then fired. Iron Eyes watched through the circle of gunsmoke as his bullet hit the horse in the head. The sound of the skull shattering echoed around him. The horse toppled like a felled oak. Its hind legs twitched.

Iron Eyes pushed his gun back into his belt and then pulled his Bowie knife from his boot neck. He moved quickly through the tall grass to the dead creature, slid the blade of the knife under the leather laces behind the cantle and cut the saddle-bags free. He unbuckled both satchels and searched them. It did not take long before he found what he had been looking for. A box of bullets and a full bottle of mezcal.

Iron Eyes smiled.

Like the ghost many claimed him to be, the bounty hunter retraced his steps through the gunsmoke back to the wagon.

Unlike the others up at the caves, Dan Landon had been unable to rest since the bounty hunter had driven the weathered wagon down to their homes. The thought of Iron Eyes razing their homes to the ground would not go away. He was tired but unable even to consider going to sleep. Not this night. He wanted to help the seriously injured Iron Eyes.

This was his and the others' fight and yet Iron Eyes had taken it upon himself to venture back into the jaws of death alone.

Why?

The question had haunted him for hours. Could it be that the bounty hunter was acting on their behalf because he was simply grateful to them for tending his wounds and giving him a little broth?

Would anyone risk their lives for a bowl of broth?

Landon had heard the gunfire moments earlier and it had drawn him away from the others. Most were already asleep and had not even heard the shots ringing out through the trees, but he had.

The big man clenched both fists and stared out

into the darkness. He felt helpless. Just because the bounty hunter had told them all to remain at the foot of the cliffs, did that mean he had to obey?

Iron Eyes had implied that if they did not have guns they could not fight. Landon raised his powerful hands and stared at his muscular arms. Even starlight did not make them appear any less dangerous.

He had never needed a gun or rifle to settle his battles before. His strength and ability to use that strength had always seen him through in the past. Why not now?

Landon knew that he could snap a man in half with his arms. Some folks did not require guns, he thought.

At last the big dirt farmer realized that he could no longer remain here like a helpless old woman. Landon snorted like a raging bull. He moved to the small pile of belongings he and his wife had brought from the cabin. He reached down and plucked his long-handled axe from the ground.

He stared at the sharpened edge of its blade. This was a weapon, if he used it as a weapon.

'You might not want any help, Iron Eyes,' he muttered. 'But you're sure gonna get it anyways.'

Axe in hand, he quickly marched into the trees. Whether the bounty hunter liked it or not, Dan Landon was determined to help him.

But the big man was not alone on his way down the trail back to the cabin. If he had taken a fraction of a heartbeat to glance over his broad shoulder he would have spotted someone following him.

Like all sons who worship their fathers, little Billy was shadowing his father's every step.

Both were rushing down into the ravenous jaws of death. One willingly. The other innocently.

Somewhere out in the centre of the valley more than thirty vaqueros were driving their horses on at increased pace to where they thought they had heard the shots coming from. Their whips and spurs were closing down the distance between themselves and their unknown enemy fast. But where in the fertile tree-covered northern end of the valley was that enemy? Finding a needle in a haystack would have proved easier but soon they would be given a fiery clue.

A guiding beacon towards which to aim their mounts.

Yet who were the hunters and who was the hunted? Were the vaqueros led by Don Miguel Sanchez hunting down their foe or was it actually Iron Eyes who was luring them into a deadly trap? A trap which could only be set by an expert hunter. Either way more blood would soon be spilled in the valley.

So much blood its creek would flow red.

There was still an awful lot of night left and the bounty hunter intended to use it to his advantage. Smoke might be OK during the hours of daylight but when the sky was black only one thing could draw human prey better.

Fire.

For since man had first learned how to make fire it had taken on an almost hypnotic quality in his soul. Iron Eyes knew that only too well. If you wanted to catch yourself a man in the dark nothing would draw him like a fire.

Iron Eyes stood beside the wagon he had driven down from the distant caves and led the palomino stallion away from between its traces. He walked the mount to the rear of Dan Landon's cabin and secured its reins to a sturdy tree. Having outdrawn the three vaqueros close to the cabin Iron Eyes now had five guns and enough ammunition to fend off a hundred men. But the vaqueros' weapons were .45s and far heavier than his own prized Navy Colts.

Too heavy for his old trail-coat pockets. There was only one way to carry this type of gun without the burden of holsters, he mused. That was to tie string to each of the guns' trigger guards and suspend them round his neck. Iron Eyes could find no string, but he decided to trim strips of leather from his saddle-bags with his Bowie knife. It took less than five minutes for the bounty hunter to complete his task.

He moved away from the stallion with the three .45s hanging from a crude leather noose. The guns dangled at the same level as his Navy Colts in his belt.

In all his years of killing, Iron Eyes had never before attempted to take on so many foes as the number he knew were after his hide now. If tackling outlaws were battles then this had to be a war.

Could one man alone win a war?

The thin figure who moved back to the wagon had no doubts that it was possible. The odds were against him but he had always managed to defeat the odds.

Iron Eyes knew that most men feared death and that gave him the edge on them. For him, death held no fear. It had ridden on his shoulder his entire life.

He had already removed the five small barrels of black powder and rolled them up to the cabin door forty feet away from the four-wheeled vehicle. From inside the cabin he found the Landons' only coal-oil lamp. He poured its meagre contents over the weathered flatbed. Its dry wood soaked the oil up like a sponge. He then added half the bottle of mezcal before consuming the rest of the fiery liquor. Again he chewed on the worm.

A twisted smile crossed his face in anticipation of what was soon to follow.

For now it was time to set his plan into action. Time for the spider to spin his web. The emaciated bounty hunter gathered up as much dry kindling as he could find in the small clearing and loaded it on top of the flatbed. To this he added every blanket he could find inside the small Landon home.

Iron Eyes glanced upward at the cloudless star-filled sky and pushed a cigar between his teeth. The alcohol had warmed up his innards enough for him to forget the nagging pain in his side.

He pulled a match from one of his deep coat-pockets and ran a thumbnail across its tip. It burst into flame. He sucked the smoke deep into his lungs and then stared at the stick of golden flickering fire between his finger and thumb. Then he tossed the match on to the kindling and blankets and watched as the flames spread across the wagon. The oil and mezcal turned the flames blue as they spread out like a living creature.

Iron Eyes knew that within a matter of seconds the fire would engulf the entire body of the wagon and send its flames higher than even the tallest of the surrounding trees.

The heat forced him back until he was standing beside the barrels of black powder. He could feel his skin blistering as the fire turned into an inferno. It felt good to have the cold driven out of his bones.

He leaned over and made a hole in the top of one of the barrels. He then grabbed it and started off down through the brush, leaving a trail of the deadly black powder behind him. He repeated this task four more times until he had each of the barrels placed exactly where he wanted it.

The bounty hunter knelt and placed the first keg down on its side, so that the trail of powder led straight to the small hole in the wooden top. He turned and looked at the flames which were already rising higher than trees in the valley. A myriad crimson sparks floated over the area like crazed fireflies.

'I reckon that ought to bring 'em on in.' Iron Eyes sucked on the cigar deep before slowly allowing the grey smoke to drift from between his teeth. 'Yep. It'll bring 'em just like moths to a flame.'

Iron Eyes was right.

He was a hunter who knew his chosen prey well.

A towering funnel of raging fire spewed upward like water from a whale's spout. It rose up into the blackness until it appeared to be touching the very stars scattered across the vast heavens. A stunned Sanchez hauled rein and stopped his powerful white charger. The most powerful man within a hundred square miles steadied his stallion whilst his vaqueros gathered around their transfixed paymaster.

'Look, amigos,' Sanchez insisted. 'We have found them.'

Luis Fernandez drew his own mount level with the Spaniard and leaned across the distance between them. Unlike his fellow riders, Fernandez knew the truth of what had happened to Pedro Ruiz. He knew that they were not hunting down a bunch of back-shooting settlers. There was only one man who mattered out there. One deadly soul who had the ability to kill with a solitary bullet.

'It is a trick,' he said.

Sanchez glared briefly at the vaquero. 'I am not a fool, Luis. I know it is a trick but that is exactly why we shall defeat them.'

'We must not be drawn to that fire, Don Miguel,' Fernandez said wisely. 'The man who killed Pedro is trying to lure us into his gun sights.'

Sanchez looked at Fernandez again. It was the look men always cast upon those whom they believe to be cowards. His eyes then returned to the flames.

'Man? We are not hunting a man, Luis. We are hunting a stinking gang of trespassers.'

Fernandez gathered his reins. 'It is a trap.'

'Of course,' Sanchez agreed. 'I am aware of that but unlike you I am unafraid because we are many and they are few. No trap can be big enough to ensnare us all.'

Another of the vaqueros known simply as Renaldo moved his horse closer to the white stallion.

'Why would the vermin set such a fire, Don Miguel?'

'To trick us of course, Renaldo,' Sanchez retorted. 'But we shall not fall for such a childish trick. I shall lead half of you straight towards those flames and the rest of you will circle around behind the fire. They will be surrounded. We shall see who it is who becomes trapped.'

Fernandez looked back at the fire. 'But the light

of the flames will make us easy targets. We shall be cut down before we ever reach them.'

Sanchez dismissed the notion. He dragged his reins hard to his right and stared straight up at the flames. The vaqueros looked at their leader as the reflected light danced in his cruel eyes.

'Renaldo will take half of you that way,' Sanchez pointed. 'The rest will follow me. We shall spread out once we are in the woods. We shall massacre them all. Their heads shall adorn the high walls of my hacienda.'

There was no time for arguments. Men like Don Miguel Sanchez never listened to anyone but themselves anyway. The riders split into two equal groups and then spurred their mounts hard into action. The vaqueros rode through the shallow creek and then began to separate as Sanchez had ordered. Their thoroughbred mounts headed straight towards the beacon of flames as their masters continued to spur them on.

They swarmed like a cavalry charge into the morass of trees in search of their sacrifices. Their weapons were primed for the forthcoming slaughter.

An invisible gauntlet had been thrown down. Sanchez had valiantly responded to the challenge.

But unknown to the vaqueros leader there was a ghostly figure awaiting their attack with even more anticipation. Waiting to unleash his own form of retribution.

Iron Eyes was ready and eager for the conflict to begin.

They had no idea that he had already declared war.

SEVENTEEN

The small boy had silently trailed his father all the way from the caves without detection. His small bare feet had taken three steps to every one stride of the huge man he worshipped. Then Billy saw the back of their cabin illuminated by the fire behind its simple form and became afraid of what lay beyond. He dropped down into the high grass and hid. But as with all fearful creatures he was unable to subdue his youthful curiosity. His large eyes and soup-basin haircut remained just above the vegetation. Billy watched.

Oblivious of the eyes on his back, Dan Landon moved along through the woods at his best pace towards the twisting spirals of flame which lit up the small clearing where his cabin stood. The closer he got the more he realized that it was the wagon that Iron Eyes had set alight and not his home. His huge frame moved down past the nervous and exhausted palomino stallion tethered beside the cabin and out into cleared area. He had barely focused upon what remained of the wagon when he felt the cold gun barrel at his neck. He paused and then looked to his side and saw the brutal features of the bounty hunter.

'Ya gonna get ya head blown off one of these days, Dan.'

'Git that gun out of my face.' Landon brushed the gun aside and glared at the man who appeared even more horrific in the dancing light of the fire. 'I came to help you.'

Iron Eyes lowered the weapon and edged to Dan's side. He saw the axe firmly gripped in Dan's huge left hand. He nodded.

'I knew you'd come to help me,' Iron Eyes said.

'How'd you know?'

'Men like you can't do nothing else but help other folks.'

'Give me one of them guns you got there.' Landon pointed at one of the .45s hanging from around the neck of the bounty hunter. 'I can pull a trigger just like any other man.'

Without even a hint of arguement, Iron Eyes pulled one of the vaqueros' Colts free of the leather lace which held it. He pushed it into the farmer's free hand and forced a grin.

'Ya got guts, Dan. Them other farmin' varmints are yella through and through.'

Landon stared at the weapon in his hand. His lips went dry and he tried to lick them but there was no spittle.

'Maybe I'm just the loco one,' he suggested.

146

Iron Eyes went to reply when something stopped him. His senses had been alerted. He stepped away from his friend. His keen instincts told him that the riders he and Landon had spotted earlier were close. They were coming from all directions.

Landon was about to speak when he heard the sound of the vaqueros' horses as they were being forced through the untamed woodland which surrounded them. His head swung around as he tried to make out the position of the men he feared.

'Riders,' Landon whispered.

'Yep. A lot of riders,' Iron Eyes agreed.

'Where are they?'

'All around us by the sound of it,' Iron Eyes muttered in a low drawl. 'We gotta make sure they don't get lost, Dan. C'mon.'

The startled farmer found himself following his thin companion towards the burning embers of the fire. Iron Eyes turned and looked hard into the big man's face.

'Git as much wood as ya can find and pile it on to these ashes, Dan. Dry or damp. It don't matter none. I want them vaqueros here.'

Landon did not argue. He pushed the gun into his belt and rushed to the edge of the clearing. He found plenty of dead wood and cut more branches with his axe. Within a few minutes he had piled enough wood on to the fire to get it burning feverishly once more.

The sound of firewood crackling filled the

clearing as Landon walked quickly to the side of the silent Iron Eyes. Sparks rose into the air and drifted downwind.

Iron Eyes grabbed the arm of his companion and then edged away from the light of the renewed blaze. A shadow at the side of the cabin gave them cover as the bony hands pulled both his Navy Colts from his belt and cocked them.

'Is this how you planned it?' Landon asked.

'Kinda.'

'But what can we do if we're surrounded?'

'We are surrounded, Dan,' the bounty hunter told him. 'Them bastards are all around us right now.'

'What?' Landon felt his heart start to pound inside his broad chest. He cast his gaze at the brush and trees all around them. Vainly he tried to see them. 'Are you sure they're all around us?'

Iron Eyes nodded. 'Yep.'

Then a chilling sound erupted. It was the collective noise of the riders as they made their final charge through the trees towards the small isolated cabin. Landon's head moved back and forth as he looked out from the shadows and saw the vaqueros force their mighty horses into the small clearing. He did not know what to do and he stared at the face of Iron Eyes beside him. There was no sign of emotion upon the scarred features of Iron Eyes.

More horsemen appeared from behind the pair. Iron Eyes dragged his companion down until they were both kneeling beside a bush. The vaqueros rode past them without seeing the two men.

'What we gonna do?' Landon whispered frantically into the ear of the silent Iron Eyes.

The bounty hunter tilted his head and smiled. 'You ain't gonna do nothing 'cept hang on to that axe and gun. Me? I'm gonna kill me a whole bunch of heathens.'

Dan Landon's powerful right hand gripped the bounty hunter's thin wrist. He held Iron Eyes in check and pulled him closer. 'I came here to help you. Damn it all. Let me help.'

'OK.' Iron Eyes gave a slow nod and felt the mighty fingers release their hold on his wrist. As Dan's head turned to look at the gathering riders less than twenty feet from where they knelt, Iron Eyes swiftly raised one of his weapons and clubbed it hard across the farmer's head. Landon slumped down to the ground at the bounty hunter's side. 'Sorry about that, Dan. But there ain't no way I can let ya get killed.'

Iron Eyes covered the unconscious figure over with leaves and then moved away. The bounty hunter crawled like a snake through the brush on his belly until he was behind trees and the horsemen who had filled the clearing.

His eyes narrowed as they focused upon them. They all had their guns drawn for action but could not locate anyone to unleash their lead fury on.

It was obvious to Iron Eyes who the leader of this

149

well-armed group of men was. Don Miguel Sanchez stood out from the other horsemen like a sore thumb. The white charger beneath him was adorned with more silver on its saddle than Iron Eyes had ever seen before. Yet for all his evident wealth he was no wiser than any of his vaqueros. The expression on Sanchez's face was exactly the same as that on those who surrounded him. They were exactly as the bounty hunter had hoped they would be. Sanchez and his men were utterly confused.

Iron Eyes placed both his Navy Colts down on the grass before him and took stock of the situation.

With cold accuracy his keen eyesight soon calculated how many of them there were. Thirty-two. Most men would have shied away from such an overwhelming force of evil but not Iron Eyes. For he had already set out the kegs of black powder around the area. All he had to do was ignite the trails of black powder with the glowing red tip of a smouldering cigar.

Iron Eyes felt for a cigar in his pocket. He gripped it between his teeth, lit it and picked up his Navy Colts. He pushed them deep into his trail coat pockets. Then, slowly, he began to crawl once more through the brushwood. He slithered between the saplings and stouter trees until he was within a mere ten feet of the blazing fire that Landon had earlier renourished with more branches.

The middle of the fire was white-hot.

He stopped and carefully got up on to his knees.

150

The vaqueros were well spread out. Some had dismounted and were searching the cabin. Another had found the palomino.

Iron Eyes knew that he had to act quickly before they also found the unconscious dirt farmer hidden on the other side of the log cabin. He pulled out the cardboard box filled with bullets for the vaqueros .45s and removed its top. He gradually rose to his feet until he was at his full height. The fire was still fearsome as its flames consumed the fresh wood.

Iron Eyes held the box of bullets in his right hand and leaned as far back as he could. Then he swung his arm like a coiled spring and watched as the box hurtled through the air. It landed in the very heart of the blazing fire.

None of the vaqueros had noticed a thing. Iron Eyes edged back behind the tree and rested his spine against its rugged bark. He drew his Navy Colts again and waited.

He did not have to wait long.

Suddenly, no more than twenty seconds after the box had landed in the fire's white-hot centre the blistering heat started to make the bullets explode. Deadly shots burst out in all directions from the flames.

Iron Eyes listened to the screams of the men and animals who were caught in the lethal barrage. Then he made his move and ran out from the cover of the trees with both guns in his hands. So many of

them had already fallen. Horses were pawing at the
air with hoofs as terror and lead cut into them. The
vaqueros were still stunned as at least a third of their
number fell from the bullets which the fire
expelled.

With cold exactness, Iron Eyes blasted one gun
after another in turn. Men were lifted from their
saddles as deadly bullets cut them down. Within a
few seconds less than half of the vaqueros were left.
Ignoring the return fire, Iron Eyes continued to
pick off his targets. Sanchez was screaming out
orders as his own mount was hit by bullets erupting
from the middle of the flames behind him. As
Sanchez hit the ground beside his stricken mount
he realized that none of his band of hired gunmen
was either listening or obeying.

Fewer than ten of the vaqueros still remained
astride their horses. They turned their animals and
spurred. Iron Eyes threw himself to the side as the
horsemen thundered past him in the direction of
the creek.

Only when he had pushed one of his guns back
into his pants belt did Iron Eyes remove the cigar
from his teeth and run across the clearing, which
was now filled with the dead and dying.

Roughly twelve yards from the flames the black
powder trails of the five kegs met. He dropped the
smouldering cigar into the powder. A plume of
smoke engulfed him for a second. Then he watched
as five trails of smoke sped away from him. It was

like watching locomotives race through the darkness into the woods.

Then the ground shook.

The entire area lit up as though it were suddenly noon. The cries of death rang out and then blackness returned. Five explosions a hundred yards down the trail had torn the fleeing horsemen apart just as Iron Eyes had planned.

Then a sound of a bullet rang out from behind him. It went through the tails of his long, tattered coat and creased the side of his bony left leg. Iron Eyes spun on his heels and saw Sanchez standing amid the bodies of men and horses alike. Smoke trailed from the barrel of his gun.

'You are the Devil.' Sanchez screamed loudly. 'But I, Don Miguel Sanchez, shall kill even the Devil. No stinking gringo can do this and live.'

Faster than the blink of an eye, Iron Eyes raised the gun in his hand and squeezed its trigger. To his horror the gun was empty. His eyes flashed at the leader of the vaqueros. Sanchez was smiling. Iron Eyes could see the thumb hauling back the hammer of the gun as it was levelled straight at him.

Like the Grim Reaper Sanchez began to walk slowly towards his chosen prey, defying the bounty hunter to try and draw one of his weapons before he squeezed his own trigger.

'Not so brave now, are you?' Sanchez mocked. 'The Devil is a coward. Don Miguel Sanchez will rebuild his empire and be even stronger than I was before. Go for those guns if you have the courage.'

'Ya don't scare me.' Iron Eyes allowed the empty Navy Colt to fall from his hand. Then he flexed his fingers. He wondered if he could grab one of his guns and fire it before Sanchez squeezed that trigger.

The gun was aimed straight at his midriff. Iron Eyes knew that the man was far too close for his bullet to miss even his thin torso.

Iron Eyes lowered his head.

He had to try to draw one of the guns, he told himself. Then he heard a sound which caused him to look up. It also caused Sanchez to stop in his tracks.

Iron Eyes looked through the strands of long hair which hung before his eyes. To his horror he saw the small child standing beside the cabin wall. Billy Landon had been scared by the sound of the explosions and gunfire, but concern for his father and the mysterious bounty hunter had forced him to break cover.

'Iron Eyes?' Billy called out. 'Where's my daddy?'

Distracted by the youthful voice, Sanchez looked over his shoulder and saw the boy. It was the last thing he would ever see.

Swiftly, the bounty hunter grabbed both the .45s which hung from around his neck. He cocked their hammers and then fired both weapons straight at Sanchez. The vaqueros' leader was lifted off the ground by the sheer power of the bullets. Iron Eyes continued to fire the guns until he had emptied all twelve bullets into the lifeless man.

'Where's my daddy?' Billy sobbed.

Iron Eyes strode through the dead and plucked the boy off the ground. He carried him to where Dan Landon was lying among the leaves.

'What's wrong with him?'

'Ya pa bin having himself a little sleep, Billy.'

FINALE

The smell of death was everywhere. Even the aroma of the strong cigar and the smoke which still rose from the smouldering ashes could not mask its putrid bouquet. The palomino stallion was wide-eyed and nervous as its new master prepared it for another long trek. Iron Eyes secured the cinch straps and unhooked the stirrup from the saddle horn. He lowered the fender and pulled the reins free of the tree at the side of the cabin before leading the animal back to where the entire community had returned. The tall bounty hunter had not spoken a word since he had dispatched the vaqueros and their brutal leader.

Eventually he stopped and looked at them. The three farmers and their families had been unable to believe what had confronted them as the sun had risen to greet another day. There were so many bodies to be seen and even more that were yet to be found.

Iron Eyes looked at Landon who was sitting on the stump of the tree outside his cabin door nursing his sore head. Wilma and Billy stood to either side of the large man. A crooked smile crossed the face of the bounty hunter as he gathered up the reins in his skeletal hands and paused beside the side of the large mount.

'Why'd you hit me, Iron Eyes?' Landon managed to ask.

'I had to hit ya,' Iron Eyes sighed as he lifted his left boot and poked it into the stirrup. 'This bunch would have shot ya for sure if I'd let ya stand by my side.'

Landon screwed up his eyes. 'How'd you figure that?'

'Easy.' Iron Eyes eased himself up on top of the palomino and held the reins in his left hand. 'Even the worst shot in the world couldn't miss a critter as big as you are, Dan.'

Landon forced himself up and stood beside the horse. He looked up at the rider.

'How'd you manage to kill them all?'

'I had a little help.' Iron Eyes glanced down at the boy who stood beside his mother.

Landon looked to where Iron Eyes was staring. 'You mean Billy helped you?'

'Yep.' Iron Eyes pulled the reins gently to his left and steadied the skittish stallion. He looked at the bodies of men and horses scattered around. 'Ya oughta clean that up before it gets too ripe, Dan.'

Landon placed a hand on the saddle. 'Hold up there. How did my Billy help you, Iron Eyes?'

The bounty hunter gave the boy another fleeting glance. 'He called out for you and made that Sanchez bastard take his eyes off me for a couple of seconds. That was time enough for me to get the drop on him. Thank ya kindly, Billy.'

'You're welcome, Iron Eyes,' Billy Landon replied from behind his mother's apron.

Landon released his grip. 'Tell me something. Do you figure them vaqueros will be back?'

'There ain't enough of them left to bother you folks none, Dan. But if I was you I'd gather up all their guns and ammunition and share it out just in case some other varmints come to rustle ya off this land.'

'Where you going?' Landon asked. 'You need to rest up for a couple of weeks.'

'I've got me an outlaw to catch and kill, Dan,' Iron Eyes stated firmly. 'I can't afford to waste time resting up.'

The burly farmer could see the five Mexican canteens hanging from the saddle horn. 'You make sure that you fill those up with water at the creek before you head off into the desert again. You hear?'

Iron Eyes nodded. 'I'll fill three of them up with water but I'll leave the other two alone.'

'Why?'

'They're full of mezcal, Dan.' Iron Eyes swung

the stallion full circle and tapped his spurs. 'I kinda salvaged it from some of them dead horses' bags.'

'What about vittles?'

'I ain't got much of an appetite at the moment,' Iron Eyes said. He slowed the mount as he passed the small wide-eyed boy. 'See ya, pard.'

Little Billy waved a small hand. 'Bye.'

Dan raised a muscular arm and waved. 'Thank you.'

There was no reply.

The fearsome rider balanced in his stirrups and whipped the shoulders of the palomino with the ends of his long reins. They all watched as the bounty hunter thundered into the dense woodland.

The war was over.

Iron Eyes was gone.